Table of Contents

You Aren't

So Bad

By
Merri Grace Bradford

Started Date: 6/23/16
Finished Date: 10/19/16
Words: 37,825

Description

Throughout the story, Embril gets beaten through difficult times. You may be surprised when I tell you that Embril does not have many friends in life. The message in the story is that you do not need friends to get through life; through the hard, easy, difficult or fun times, but it doesn't hurt to have friends in the first place.

Thanks to Nanny, Papaw,
Nickie, and friends.

Chapter One

The Library Door was only three feet away now. I stopped to take one last look before exiting this room until what felt like eternity-tomorrow. The room was in the form of a circle which made you dizzy if you looked at it for too long. The shelves were stacked high to the ceiling with hundreds of books filling every tiny space. There were a few tables in the room, some with four chairs, and some with two. The wooden theme of the library was so beautiful, I realized that I could live in this room for the rest of my life, but this isn't marriage. I sighed.

In a normal library, you would see stickers telling you which kind of books were in a particular section of the room. Instead, there was a poster that hung to the right of the door as you walked in that looked somewhat like a map. That was my favorite part, that a human wouldn't be treated like a child, the human would have to look at the map and figure out where to look. I couldn't promise you that you would find the exact book you wanted, but I'm sure that you couldn't leave without one.

The book in my hand now was written by John Green, The Fault In Our Stars. It's supposed to be about a girl who is fighting cancer and meets a guy named Augustus Waters in their support group, when they fall in love. What an unusual but heart tearing thought. I suddenly wished that I could be as good a writer as John Green. I want to make people go on an insane, emotional roller-coaster that makes them question their actions. My teachers always read the stories I've written outside of class and tell me I am naturally talented, but I always miss something.

With a sigh, I turned back to the door and walked out of my beautiful library. When I entered the kitchen, Mom was cooking dinner by the stove, which got my heart pounding.

"Mom, what are you cooking? That smells amazing!"

"Chicken, rice and broccoli," she answered all smug and proud.

I walked on over to where she was and stood looking over her shoulder so I could smell it better. She decided that wasn't enough for a first conversation of the day so she added, "What did you do today?"

"The usual," I paused to roll my eyes, she should know, "Finished a book so I found another one."

My mom drew in a quick breath and I could tell she was trying to hide her thoughts from me, that I shouldn't lock myself in that library all the time, that I should be out with friends, I really don't have any friends anymore, I can't help it if I'm in love with the place!

"Embril, Billy built that room for everyone in the family, not just you," she had to go there. She used my name and Billy's in the same sentence. Billy is my great-grandfather, sadly he died from Alzheimer's disease but in the pictures I've seen, he didn't look like the kind of person I'd be hanging out with all the time.

"Mom, who else uses it?"

"Your father; myself."

"Okay."

"When you have the time", I added in my head.

Andrew uses it sometimes but I can almost guarantee that he's only in there for his school projects. My brother reads books but only when he feels like it or also, has the time. He works at this local pull in food place called Sonic. Sometimes we pull in just to laugh at Andrew but we get food too, its mostly fried but still delicious. My brother, Andrew, is almost always at work, but honestly I don't think that would get in anyone's way of reading.

Without any more words, I walked upstairs to my room and threw myself on my queen size bed. The sheets are light blue to match my walls and they smell like the ocean. I buried my face into the sheets and shook my head left and right until I laughed at myself for acting so stupid. Then I sat up right and pulled out my phone from my pocket. There were two missed calls from Kali, my

Dad's mom. So I pressed the call back button and cleared my throat so I could talk clearly.

"Hello?"

"Howdy Nanny."

"What are you up to?"

"You called me?" did I have to ask?

"Yes, I am going to the library tomorrow. I know you like to read so do you want to come with me?"

Ahhh! Of course there isn't any other way I'd want to spend time with my Nanny, Kali, but I just found a new book and I don't want to see anything that will make me question my choice. I hesitated to say no, because I thought I might hurt her feelings so I told her sure and hung up so she wouldn't hear the muffled sound of me screaming into my sheets.

When I heard the faintest yell of Mom calling my name I stopped the unnecessary scream and ran downstairs counting them as I went.

"Yes?" I asked, but no one was to be seen. I was going to holler for her, but nothing settles a *No I wasn't just screaming into my ocean smelling sheets because of the plans I just made,* type of situation like pretending that I heard what they said.

Though I didn't hear what they told me to do, the sink looked pretty full.

Letting an "Awww," out of my mouth I walked slowly toward the dishes.

When I opened the dishwasher door, it was full of clean dishes. Another "Awww," escaped and I pulled out the top drawer. It wasn't long before I started singing the National Anthem. I'm not a good singer but that doesn't change tradition. When I was younger, Mom would do the dishes with me and we would sing this song and then it would lead to something more modern like Carrie Underwood or Taylor Swift.

I let my mind wander as I worked. I wandered why Mom wasn't in here helping and singing with me, I wondered why I was such a bad singer that even the stray cat just outside the door was squealing in terror! It seemed like I was at an opera show when my Mom joined me in song. Unlike me, she was good at it and it made me happy. Her voice made me forget I was doing chores and it seemed that we were just singing together in our own talent show, even though she was my partner in doing chores. I giggled at that thought hoping no one saw, even though there isn't a point of caring why I laugh at myself so much.

Before I was finished with the second song, the dishwasher was empty. I smiled to myself and smelled the bread burning in my nose.

"Mom!" I yelled. She came running and I flinched, surprised that she heard me, "Bread is burnin',"

"I know, I know, I know," she said making the last word longer than all the rest.

When she pulled the pan out I scrunched up my nose, the smell was horrid. What did she put on it!? Usually her bread is really good, perhaps she got too confident and started experimenting. I didn't want to hurt her feelings so I tried to keep my mouth closed. *Aw no is that lemon? I think she put lemon on it, what for!? No way can I keep this in.*

"Mom, Uh, is that lemon?"

"Yeah, I saw this thing on the internet that said if you put lemon juice on your bread it will turn green," she smiled and then let that drop, saddened that her experiment didn't work the way she wanted it to.

I would have asked her why she wanted it to be green but I was afraid that too would, hurt her feelings. Instead, I gave her a hug and went to the cabinet to get out the plates. When I turned around she was still frowning at the pan of now burnt, lemon-smelling,supposed-to-be-green bread.

"I'm sure it will be good anyway," I said trying to cheer her up. I didn't like her upset and Andrew is actually off work for supper.

Just then, Andrew walks in from the living room, his face confused.

"Why does it smell like . . ".

I rapidly started to shake my head to the left and the right using my right hand the opposite way of my head just under my chin telling him not to say anything or he's a dead man from me, meaning he will have to wash his hands with food coloring instead of soap for the next week.

Andrew saw Mom standing at the tiny oven and understood what I meant. Mom finally started to move and told us to go ahead and get our plates.

Andrew was the first to get in line. He took a piece of lemon bread first just in case Mom was still looking, which she wasn't, and I followed him, doing the same. I actually felt like his puppet, following every move he did, like I was too scared to go my own route. I didn't like that, because I'm normally plenty brave enough.

When I got to the rice, I noticed the cheese was a Velveeta brand she had made it with. That particular cheese brand was one that had been passed down along with the house I live in now. It was part of the recipes my Great grandmother used while she was a chef. I had seen in one of the cook books that she wrote in her own handwriting *to always use Velveeta cheese, it's the best in everything, that makes your meal tasting top notch.* I will always remember that, how she ridiculously emphasized the use for Velveeta cheese.

When we all had our plates and were sitting at the table. It took me a while to realize that we were all staring at our plates instead of eating our dinner. It was quiet, much too quiet for what a dinner should be. So, I picked up my burnt lemon bread, took a slightly deep breath because I felt eyes on me now, though my own eyes are closed. I opened my mouth and pushed the bread forward only to miss my mouth so it hit my lip instead. I heard a chuckle from Andrew beside me but I ignored him and took a bite. I felt my eyebrows grow straight up surprised by the taste. It definitely wasn't the best piece of bread I've tasted, it would probably be better if it weren't burnt but I'm still surprised, the lemon bread was shockingly good.

"Wow Mom, try some." I kept my voice low so I wouldn't give them false expectations.

When mom took a bite, so did Dad, and then Andrew. Each person took on the same facial expression I did. That made me smile.

We seemed to grow out of the silent dinner date into a talkative night. Dad asked me what book I'd jumped to. He listened while I explained and it made me that much happier that I was so blessed to have a good family. That made me remember how two years ago, when I was going into the freshmen year of high school, I told myself I didn't need friends. Tonight only made that statement much more true.

Chapter Two

My alarm was constantly beeping. I'd turned it to snooze once but that didn't help. Knowing I couldn't do anything about it, I rolled off the bed.

My head hit the floor with a thud. "Owe!" I yelled in pain. Perhaps next time I will take it slower and land upright on my big feet.

"Embril? Are you okay?" I heard my mom ask and by the way she said it, her voice seemed to be like she knew I was fine but couldn't help ask anyway. Ugh!

"Yeah!" I guess the pound of me hitting the floor was louder than I thought it was. When I finally got to my feet, I felt the blood rush to my face and my room started to swirl in circles. I tried to shake off the dizziness and get dressed for our second week of school. Junior year isn't at all what I thought it would be, it was worse. We have a new principal and he's pretty strict. Yes, we did get part of our dress-code back but that was almost like a trade, get a little better of a dress-code for a more strict principal, life couldn't get any better.

When I got downstairs, Mom was already gone. Since she had to be at work at seven I never could get downstairs in time for her to do my hair. So, I packed my lunch and grabbed a pack of crackers out the door I went.

My truck was parked on the patio instead of over by the trees where I normally park. Since Andrew used my truck to see his girlfriend yesterday, he hadn't thought to park it where it should have been. Though I don't complain, my hands were full so it made it less of a walk. I opened the back door closest to the house and threw my back pack in. The back seat is a tight space. A person my age could barely fit back there but it was possible. The windows in the back were small and you had to pull the lever and push the window out yourself if you wanted it open.

I stepped back to examine my beautiful truck crossing my fingers, if Andrew got a scratch on it, he'd have to survive the rest of the month paying it off and paying for all my gas. Thankfully, the truck was still in the perfect condition I had left it in.

The morning was unusually misty. I had to turn on my headlights just to see ten inches up the road. The ride to school was quiet and lonely-- something I didn't mind-- but still it would have been nice to have someone talk to, someone like Andrew.

★★★

Mr. Tidewalk decided to have a long and boring class. Most the time I just wished he would give us a break so I could dive into the first few pages of "The Fault In Our Stars", but I knew I had to listen. When the bell rang, everyone was in a hurry like a swarm of bees that just flew in through the window. Not me. I'm not afraid of bees. The hallway was crowded as usual, so I squirmed through crowds of people to walk to class by myself, like I did every day.

Second block wasn't as bad. When I first walked in, I took the front but farthest desk from the teacher. Michael Shrew walked in as well but in a weird way. He sat beside me and asked if that was okay. I felt like I was choking on my own saliva so I only shrugged. Michel didn't say anything else to me for the rest of the class. My English teacher told us to get a book and read quietly and I knew no one else would do what the teacher asked but I didn't care. That's why second block was so surprising, I'd always envisioned Michael as the popular kid who would sit in the back and talk. Instead, he sat there reading a book called "The Hatchet". He didn't walk to our next class with me either. He ditched me to flirt with some girl standing beside her locker.

Next was history, ugh, the worst subject invented. I was so happy when the words came across the intercom, "Students, please report to the auditorium."

The auditorium was already full by the time I had got there. That meant I had to sit by two people I had no idea of. The lights turned off and huge white screen rolled down from the top of the stage. When I realized they were showing a video about bullying, I was yearning for history class. Though I waited until they turned the

14

lights back on for me to read, from all the commotion, I was sure I'd be the *last* person to get in trouble.

When school was over, I felt like I needed food so I pulled into Sonic, where Andrew works, and bought a drink with some cheesy fries. Then I got a call from nanny so I pressed answer and put it on speaker, "Hello?"

"Hey, I was wondering if you want to go to the library now or after five?"

"Um, Now is great," I answered jumping with excitement inside.

"Okay, meet you there."

"Aright," I said trying to hide the enthusiasm in my voice, but she had already hung up.

The library was full. Not a sight a teenage girl would see everyday. I guessed there were just a lot of school projects being handed out early. Kali went straight to the computers to search for a book while I went to the fiction section. These shelves were short and not stacked up high like the ones in my library at home. I hadn't been here since I was a child so I've actually never been to the teenage or adult part of this library. What an adventure.

The first book I picked up was called The Selection series. It had a picture of a girl in a long beautiful blue dress on the front and the author was Kiera Cass. I would have read this book if it weren't for my library at home. I'd already read the entire series and everything that author wrote, I completely adore her.

The next book was another one by John Green, it was called Paper Towns. I would check it out, but there was no use, again, I had already read that book. I went along the aisle picking up random books from random people, there just wasn't one I didn't have in my library, perhaps this place isn't as interesting as I thought it was, or maybe they can't find any new books to buy.

When I came across the computers again, I noticed a new girl sitting in one of the chairs. Her hair was long and blond and she sat up so straight it made my back hurt just looking at her.

When she turned her head around I ducked behind a random shelf hoping she didn't see me. Then I lifted my head just a little to see her. I know her! Her name is Clara Arattingburg. She was on the soccer team for school and I remember I was forced to speak to her because our teacher assigned us as partners last year. She isn't a bad person just extremely lazy for a use-to-be soccer player, it got on my nerves and I had to do most the work. The good thing is, she never lied about what she did and didn't do. Even though I knew who she was, I still waited for her to turn her head so I could stand up and go find Nanny.

When I did stand up, I didn't have to look, Kali was standing right behind me as I slowly stood up to meet her gaze.

"Are you ready?" she asked, like she was mad at me.

"Yes, I couldn't find anything," I said tilting my head down.

Without saying anything else she turned and headed for the check out center with me right behind her.

★★★

I pulled into the driveway with ease. Mom's car was home, but not Andrew's. My dad was home too, so I parked back at the patio. I've decided to keep this spot as my new parking area, but only until I get in trouble for parking there. The truck came to an abrupt stop when I slammed on the breaks. My mind was too busy wondering about getting in trouble to notice that I was about to hit Dad. Then I got out as fast as I could to explain that usually doesn't happen.

"Em, stop it you're yelling!"

I felt my jaw clam shut. No one would hear me for miles out here, even if I used a megaphone so I haven't the faintest idea why he wanted me to stop.

"Why are you outside?" I asked trying to make up for the almost accident.

"Waiting for you. Go inside, your Mom is finished cooking."

This scared me. I opened the truck door to get out my back pack and headed for the house. My Dad hasn't

16

been mad at me in so long, I don't know what I did wrong.

"Mom?" Every word was sticking in my throat, each one getting harder to speak.

"Have a seat," she said.

The tension grew, my Dad walked in, doing everything but slamming the door shut in the process. Mom brought me a plate full of baked beans, a cheeseburger and corn on the cob. I waited as Dad put food on his plate and they both finally joined me. Dad first, they started furiously stabbing at their beans with forks and shoving it into their mouth, never looking up at me. I just sat there watching them eat like pigs wishing for this to end.

"Tastes good Georgia," Dad called mom by her name. I really wish they would let me in on the inside scoop as to why are they upset?

"You're not eating Embril?" My Mom asked.

"I'd like to, but I also would like for ya'll to tell me why you are so furious with me."

I felt relief because I could get the words out and everything seemed to soften a bit, Dad's shoulders even dropped.

"Where were you?" Mom asked taking the step Dad refused to do.

"After school? Nanny asked me to go to the library with her."

Dad suddenly threw his cob on his plate which made me jump in my seat.

"There was an accident at the gas station by your school today. We were scared it was you." My mom explained, her eyes watery.

"You should have told us." Dad said.

I didn't speak. I couldn't. All I could do was to lower my head. We finished our dinner in silence. I felt so ashamed.

"I'm going to start the fire," Dad said and pushed up from the table.

I look up at Mom with confused eyes.

"Were having a bonfire tonight," her voice was calm now, soft. At least she could let something go.

After I was finished eating too, I took my plate to the sink and followed Mom out to the fire pit hoping Dad would drop the act before the night ended. We sat in a triangle but I didn't like it so I scooted over beside Mom, fearing that Dad would snap at me for staring at the fire too much.

The fire reminded me of all the bonfires I had back here when I was younger. I had friends then, it was October in 2014-2015, my seventh grade year, which was the best. We had my Dad tell ghost stories about our land back when there were Indians that lived here. Also, there were ingredients for s'mores and we had games like bobbing for apples and bean bag toss. I felt the corners of my mouth pull up to a smile, but Mom and Dad were still frowning. Suddenly everything was bad again. The silence picked back up to its normal speed and all that was left were three frowning people at the crackling fire. My phone said eight o' clock p.m.

"I'd better get to my homework," I said standing up. I got no response. It was like my parents were dazzled by the fire so much they couldn't tear their eyes away, like if we were at Disney World and fireworks suddenly danced across the sky.

My room was cold. The math problems on my paper were staring back at me. Fifteen minutes passed with me and my problems having a stare-down. This made me wish I had paid attention in first block today. A sigh that I didn't remember holding escaped from my mouth. I couldn't concentrate. My room was too cold, my Dad was mad at me, and I had no idea what tomorrow would be like. I felt lonely and depressed. When was I going to have some fun?

I looked back down to problem number three and still had no idea where to start so I packed up my work and slipped on my black Nike sandals.

There were twelve steps from story two, to story one. I'd started counting them when I was ten because walking with my eyes closed were so much more fun.

I stopped at the kitchen table, but it was suddenly too crowded for homework. I kept walking until I reached the side door. Mom and Dad were still sitting by the fire in the back so I grabbed a blanket and headed for the pond where I spent most my time as a child. You could see it from the house, but if you really wanted to you could hide behind the one tree covering the right side of the pond. So that's where I went. I sat on the ground behind the tree and curled up under my blanket. I had my math book with me too so I looked up what we were studying. I finally figured it out and wrote down every note I needed.

When my math was done I leaned my head back to get a break. Then my mind started wondering like crazy, from cleaning the house right, to being in my library reading a book, to sipping a milkshake from any local place I could think of. I closed my eyes and let my math book slide from my hand. Then I saw pitch black darkness behind my eye lids.

Chapter Three

Suddenly I was tearing through yet another Christmas present. The last two were things I'd asked for, a guitar and a series of books I'd been wanting. The second present was number one on my list, the books. I couldn't wait to add them to the library in the back of the house. We opened presents in a sequence, first was Andrew, then me, next was Dad then Mom. It was my turn again, third round. A tiny square box twirled through my fingers as I tore off the wrapping, not caring if it ripped in the process. The box was black and had a design of flowers on the outside. It was also harder than a tiny box should be. I slowly took the lid off half expecting a tiny monkey to jump through the ceiling. Really, why would such a tiny box need so much protection?

There was a silver circular ring covered in bubble wrap. I picked up the ring and took off the plastic, popping bubbles on the way. It was a charm bracelet, two charms were dangling as I held the ring in front of my eyes to examine it, one was a book, the other was a spoon. I looked up to Mom with confusion, "A spoon?"

She smiled, "Since you like to cook, it's a reminder of your ancestors, they were all chefs remember?"

I nodded, "Yep, I remember," then I thought Mom and Dad deserved a bear hug for such a thoughtful gift.

"Embril! Hey there she is. Embril!" I jumped and started looking around. I was dumbfounded not remembering this happening in the Christmas memory. Then it caught me, I wasn't really back in 2012, fifth grade. I wasn't off for the two weeks on Christmas break and this was just a memory.

Andrew had shaken me awake.

"WHY CAN'T I SLEEP?!" I shouted only half asleep.

Andrew flinched and decided it was safer to take a few steps back. I looked around until I found the sun blinding my vision. Then I was really awake. My memory was just a dream from my favorite Christmas year. That was a long time ago.

I opened my eyes all the way so I could see clearly. I was still sitting on the grass, now covered with dew, behind the tree by the pond. I guess I fell asleep. *Oh, oh. I fell aslee... school*!

"What time is it?"

Andrew hesitated to make sure I wasn't going to lunge at him and start throwing punches for waking ,(or not waking), me up.

"Andrew!"

Finally he answered, "Seven forty-four."

"Perfect, I was supposed to leave fourteen minutes ago."

"Yeah, figured I'd find you here. Mom was worried but Dad didn't really care."

"Of course he wouldn't," I mumbled under my breath not sure if he heard me.

Instead of checking, I turned and bolted for the door. My mind was scrambling trying to pick through my closet in my head, what would I wear?

I had to ignore the smell of pancakes as I ran through the kitchen, breakfast wasn't really on my mind now but it did smell good. Just smelling it made my stomach grumble but that too I had to pretend didn't exist, not at the moment.

Finally I reached my room and threw on a t-shirt and some jeans. Then I pinned my hair back and check myself in the mirror but it didn't look quite right. I needed something else. Then I was searching the top of my desk clattered with jewelry and make-up that I never wore.

"Ugh! Where is it?" I said, frantically! If that charm bracelet was gone I was sure the tears would start gushing down my face before I could attempt to hold them back. "I need it"! Stopping for a break, Andrew walked into my room in just his underwear.

"Andrew, *please* put some clothes on! I'm sure half the school wouldn't care but *please*, for me?"

It sounded more of me begging than I wanted it to. Surely he cared about my feelings more than embarrassing me by showing up to school looking like….like *that*.

He grinned, "Senior skip day."

I moaned, "Is there any way I could skip without getting in trouble? No, of course not. Was Senior skip day even at the beginning of the year? Probably not".

I turned back around to face my desk and I finally saw it, the silver bracelet was shinning off the only light bulb I had left on in my room. I took the bracelet and slipped it onto my wrist.

"Ha!" I ran past Andrew bumping his shoulder on the way. As I passed the kitchen for the second time, I grabbed a pancake and headed for my truck.

When I got to the patio, I almost screamed. My lungs were burning with fire trying to not let a single noise escape my mouth, I had no idea why, maybe because I knew I'd get a sore throat later.

"To the left," Andrew said. Apparently he had followed me out here and knew what I was looking for. I looked to the left like he said and sure enough, my truck was in its usual parking spot. I groaned and checked Andrew's face. Yep, he was laughing. I bet he thinks my frustration is hilarious. I would be planning to get him back for this if I hadn't thought he truly meant no harm. I couldn't hold anything back any more, I felt like I was about to burst into flames and let Andrew clean up my ashes, but I was disappointed because all I could let out was the littlest, "Ugh!"

I stomped over to my truck and threw my back pack into the passenger seat instead of in the back.

Sure enough, I was late to school. My first block teacher decided that he liked me and I was here every other day so he let it slide. Of course I'm thankful for that, but I sure didn't deserve it.

Then the entire class was lame and boring, he claimed it a study hall, probably giving up class for me thinking I needed sleep or something. I wanted to show him that I didn't need an excuse, and that I'm perfectly capable of getting into trouble which was actually not true unless I had no other option. I wanted to get out of my seat and scream in his face for giving me something I never earned, for drawing attention to me and now I'm certain that all the other students think I act like I'm better than them.   I want to get up and jump up and down in a temper tantrum and cross my fingers in hopes that photographers come in to watch me throw a fit and then put it all over the internet so the world can see who Embril Jack *"truly"* is. But then I thought that my teacher is one of a kind, who if you rejected their offer in any way humanly possible, they would make you're life a living nightmare. I decided it probably wouldn't look good on my record if I got expelled from school; then I wouldn't ever get into a decent college. I was absolutely furious!

I finally decided that reading would help me calm down. So, I took that route instead of trying to sleep. I opened up to chapter eight and tried to stay distracted for the rest of class, even the rest of the day.   One lesson missed out of history couldn't tear me apart. I waited for school to pass by, which surprisingly it went pretty fast.

Home was quiet. Mom tried to take a nap, Dad was outside working on something and Andrew went to the store. I had a pretty rough day. Even though it was just a plain old day, I still needed a distraction.

The library was empty. I walked in, completely ignoring the map and sat down at a two-seated table grasping my book as hard as I could. For a minute I thought I might hurt the book if I wasn't careful so I let up. Great, thinking books had feelings...now I'm really going crazy.

I haven't gotten time to read much of the book, but I wanted to get a lot in today. As soon as I opened it up, Andrew came walking in.

"Get out," he said.

"Excuse me? I was here first," I whined.

"I have friends over for a project," he paused, "So, get out."

Ugh, so reading couldn't be a distraction forever. I would've yelled back at him to find another library, but his friends weren't that bad. Though how should I know?

All my friends are lost to me, I don't have any now. So, I picked up my book and stomped out.

I couldn't find any other distraction. My parents were busy doing other things so I decided to take a trip to the store, for no apparent reason. The drive there was lonely. The radio didn't soothe me like I hoped it would. The parking lot was full of cars and people. Perfect, a place filled with people; that's the last thing I want. There are millions of opportunities here to make me more upset. Today has not been a good day.

The doors automatically opened for me to walk through. The red box, a place to rent movies, was over to my right, but I didn't want to spend money on a movie that wasn't good enough to distract me. So I passed it and kept walking until I got to the book section. They were interesting, but each book was so short that I would finish it before I went to sleep tonight, I needed one that would take my mind off things for a day or two. I need a vacation, an adventure.

When I stuck my head out from the aisle there was a guy looking at me. He had brown hair and brown eyes. He was skinny, but not thin as a toothpick. I wondered where I had seen him before but I couldn't think. My mind trailed back to the awful day I had, starting with Andrew telling me I was late for school.

I shook my head as if I was trying to clear it from my brain and stepped back inside the aisle. I decided to go out the other way and headed for the electronics. I remember seeing my Dad carry around a camera. He looked like he was having so much fun just snapping pictures of us when we would get muddy in the back yard or when we go on vacation, I wanted to try it too but he wouldn't ever let me, "You're too young," he would say, maybe now I'm old enough, if I bought him something to go with it, perhaps he would finally let me try.

When I found the cameras, the same guy that was looking at me earlier was there. It was like he read my mind and knew I would be there next. I sighed and just walked to the other aisle by the computers. I placed my hand on the shelf so that just the tips of my fingers guided along the silver shelf looking at each computer as I passed. I turned around to check the other aisle, to see if the creepy guy was still there, but this was worse. The guy was now on the same aisle I was. He was not looking at me this time, but a computer himself. I turned back around and walked faster but a cold hand touched my elbow which made me flinch and swirl back around to see the creepy guy. Was he stalking me? What did I do to him?

"Come with me I want to show you something," he said. His voice was deep, almost too deep for a teenager. He was cute, but I can't think of that now, he is probably trying to kidnap me or something.

"No!" I shrieked and tried to pull my arm away but he tightened his grip which burned my elbow.

"Ow!" I screamed, but I didn't stop trying to yank my arm away. I wanted someone to save me from this....monster! That wasn't going to happen, I was not a princess and I was alone. I was not a fictional character in a book, this was reality. The brown eyed guy loosed up jut a little but I was still in pain. *Think fast Embril*, I told myself and frantically looked around for something to help me. Then I caught a glimpse of the shelf that was broken. If I could somehow get him close enough, it could cut him.

So, I walked forward and suddenly threw my side into the shelf. It worked, his other hand swung so fast that the shelf cut his flesh. He didn't make a sound but he scrunched his face up and finally let me go free. Without looking back I bolted for the closest room I could find. I didn't want to take any chances with running, I wasn't very fast and he looked fit, I bet he runs for fun or something along that nature.

I found the girls bathroom and hoped he didn't see me. He could also be brave enough to enter if he really wanted to get to me so badly. There are so many options, so many possibilities, that I have to be open to the best idea I can think of,;which means, I need to climb out ofthe bathroom window.

I probably look like a crazy person because the bathroom was also filled with people, but I didn't care. I searched and searched for a window, but there wasn't one. Great, how did anyone escape in movies through the bathroom window if there never was any window? Instead of crawling through an air vent, I stood there in the line with everyone else. When a stall opened up I smiled and told the next person to go ahead, it was getting annoying. I checked my phone and it had already been twenty-five minutes since I came in here. Hopefully that was long enough. The door opened in front of me and it made me jump in horror, though it was just *another* girl.

I was able to make it through the rest of the store and out to the parking lot before anyone else could snatch me up and take me away. That's when I saw him again, the brown hair sticking up from his Chevy truck. It was red, the same color as mine (so he has good taste) but I didn't want to stare and draw attention to myself, so I flew open the door and started the engine.

My gas light clicked on and so did the fuse for my anger. There was no way I wanted to get gas. I hoped the gas I had would last me until I got home, which it did; though our driveway is so long, I'm not sure it will last me to get to the road for school tomorrow. I guess hope is the only thing stronger than fear. I should keep that in mind when I am fighting a familiar looking stranger.

There was nothing to help distract me from my frustrating day, even the almost disaster kidnapping. So, I climbed in bed and shut the light off.

★★★

The next day went smoother. Everything seemed simple. Of course I was still frustrated with the familiar stranger incident, but I refuse to let that hold me back, I have a life to live.

After school, I went to a Student Council meeting. Student Council is a School club that I'm in where we put things together, host and plan things for the Student Body, like prepare for Prom or Homecoming. Today we are setting up the decorations in the gym for the homecoming parade. It was fun but like I said, also lonely. I don't have a lot of people to talk to. Though, if I sat alone and talked to myself all the time, I would be front page news, so I hang around my old friends that I kind of left. I speak occasionally but no one ever responds to what I have to say. I guess I don't speak the right words. The weirdest part of decorating, was when I was painting the flag that the decorated carts would tear through when it was time to start, I spotted the same brown-haired brown-eyed guy staring at me.

So, he goes to my school and we're in the same club. That's where I knew him from, but it was still creeping me out, we're not exactly friends.

Chapter Four

Dear Embril,

When I'm in high school, I want to have read all the books in the world. I want to have ridden a pony and played the guitar, I want to have sung in a talent show with mMommy. Then maybe after that, I can write a book and own my own library.

From,

yourself.

The letter that I supposedly wrote to myself in third grade was childish, I admit. Though it was childish enough to make me laugh. My third grade teacher, Mrs. Brittney, sent this letter to me in the mail. I picked it up yesterday afternoon but I was so tired that I fell into bed without opening it. No, I have not read all the books in the world, or ridden a pony, or sang in the talent show, I'm not old enough to own my own library, but writing a book sounds like a possible goal. I've tried before, but it was never good enough to publish. As a child, I had the goal to play the guitar, at least I did that.

My smile didn't feel as big on the outside as it did internally, but I'm happy that I had already gotten one childish goal accomplished within seven years. Perhaps, that's what my book will be about.

I climbed off my bed and wandered over to my desk that held my computer. Today I decided I should just set everything up. Maybe tomorrow I could start this new adventure.

After I made several documents to help with my writing, I took my book and headed back to my bed. I actually got to read a few chapters yesterday, so now I'm on chapter fourteen. The chapter started with the two characters flying back home from Amsterdam and discussing dreams. I specifically remembered the line Hazel said, "Ignorance is bliss." Ain't that true?

The word ain't reminded me of how Mom, Dad, Andrew and I went to family night at our grandparents house, only two weeks ago. We made a new game, we had to speak all words in the most country-like form all the way though dinner. If you spoke normal once, you were out, but none of us lost that game.

I tilted my head back down to what I was reading. Then something odd happened. This cloudy, but smoky smell filled my lungs. It smelled like a fire was burning, but then again I was reading a book, so I thought my nose was playing tricks on me. When the smell didn't go away, I stopped reading to make sure this was reality. The smell got stronger and stronger, until my door caught on flames. That brought me to this moment.

I yanked my phone charger from the wall and grabbed my phone. I need something to put it in, some type of emergency kit. I remembered that when I was a child, I put together a safety bag in case of an emergency. I scrambled in my brain to remember where I put it. Under the bed. When I pulled the bag out I hit my head. Then the world started to spin around me so fast that I couldn't keep up with it. Then I felt myself toppling over to the right just before everything turned black.

★★★

When I opened my eyes I started to panic. What's going on? I scrambled to my feet and that's when I smelled smoke. Is my house on fire?

I saw the bag in my hands and directly knew what I had been doing, but I don't remember how this happened.

I opened the bag to find water and crackers inside, that were probably no good by now. Then I threw my phone and my charger in the bag. Next I grabbed my book from my bed and slung the bag over my shoulder.

It felt like I was stumbling and tripping over things on my floor as I reached for my door knob.

My vision was getting blurry and the closer I got to the door, the hotter it became, which irritated my nose and my throat and made me cough.

I tried to be careful, afraid my pants would catch fire in an instant. Finally, I got my fingertips on the knob of the door, I pulled back a little too quickly, so my fingers completely slipped. The knob was so hot it was burning my fingers. I don't care, a little burn is better than dying, I grabbed the door knob with my entire palm and twisted until the door flew open. Instead of walking or crawling out, I back pedaled slowly from the door.

I looked around to see that my room was completely clean, I had been stumbling over my own two feet. The fire crawled in faster than I ever would have expected. I tried to breathe, I wanted that to soothe me, to help me calm down, but it onlymade things worse. The smoke piled up which made the air thick and hard to breathe. Besides, my head was starting to throb from when I hit it on the bed.

Firefighters had told me to crawl through the smoke out of your door, if your house caught on fire, but I couldn't do that. My nightstand caught on fire next, which made me flinch. I stood there and watched the flames run alongside brutally murdering the wood. I wanted to stay. I wanted to sit down on *my* floor, I wanted to hug my knees and curl up into a ball. I wanted to stay and burn with my house, I didn't want to abandon my own home. I wanted to tell myself it wasn't real and burn up into ashes with it, and the next day everything would be okay, I wouldn't be lost. Knowing my bed would catch on fire next, I couldn't stand and watch, it would be too painful, so I ran.

The only other exit I had was my window. Hesitantly, I pushed it up and forced my legs through the tiny space, suddenly feeling weak. I shut off all my thoughts and my brain completely, then slid to the end of the slopped roof. My eyes were closed but I couldn't stay up here forever, the roof would eventually collapse too. Instead of opening my eyes like a normal human being would, I jumped, with my eyes still closed.

★★★

I felt like a character in a book. I felt all the true pain happening but it felt like it wasn't real. That I really could have curled into a ball on my floor and be undamaged. Though none of this happened, my house *was* on fire. My brother caught me instead of letting me hit the ground and pass out like I half way hoped I would. My family had all gotten outside okay. I was the last, I guess books really do take you for a spin.

We had backed up into the trees. I was supposed to feel safe. To feel happy because I wasn't where the danger was. Actually I was right there in the middle of it. I didn't feel safe and protected, I felt useless and like a terrible person, like I abandoned my family. That's what my house is to me, it's my family. I looked down to my wrist. The bracelet was there, I never took it off. Perhaps this is my good-luck charm.

When I looked back up to my burning house, I was scared for it. I was sad. My bracelet reminded me of all the Christmases we had, all of the times we cooked as a family and brought our pet frogs into the house, though I couldn't remember all of each story.

Suddenly, a strange feeling flew in. My inside was flooding, filling up with water, no, not water...panic! Where would we hide from the bad guys? How would we cook our chicken and stay dry from the rain?

Then I found myself running again. I was running back toward the house. My memories were locked up inside there, in with the danger. The house was the only thing in my family that knew all the memories I couldn't remember forever. I was afraid I would never get those memories back and the house would be forgotten along with those memories, my house would forget me. The fire would take them all up and destroy them one room at a time. I was running back inside to find those memories, to save them before it was too late.

Two gigantic arms wrapped around my waist pulling me back and I heard my name being yelled into my right ear. It was Andrew, he was screaming as loud as he could, "Embril stop! Embril! I will not lose my only sister! Embril stop fighting!"

I let go. If the house lost its memories...so would I. My muscles loosened. Andrew's didn't, his arms tightened like I was tricking him and would bolt again at any given moment. He dragged me back to the rest of the family where Mom pulled me into a bear hug and Dad kissed my hair. When I was trusted enough be let go, I stood with my family in the woods. We stood alone, forced to watch the only home we've had fall and crumble. We were helpless.

I turned to look Andrew in the face, but he wouldn't let me, he continued to look down as I spoke, "I'm sorry," I said holding back the tears that threatened to come. Andrew never answered so I looked away and to the ground as well.

"Embril...what were you doing before this happened?"

It felt like a punch in the gut. My own mother was accusing me for starting the fire. How could she? And now of all times she thinks its best to figure out how it happened? Honestly, I don't care, I don't want to know.

"I was reading," I said. Then it was quiet until I spoke aloud what I was thinking. "Books bring out your inner mind and you go into someone else's created world. They take you to a different place. So the one thing I urge you to do when reading....is to figure out what is reality and what is imaginary."

Chapter Five

We were still standing back by the woods. The tears I had asked not to come, came anyway. My face felt sticky with salt and my eyes felt swollen. It was hard to keep my eyes open and it had been silent for quite a while.

When I heard the first words since I had last spoke, I looked up to Dad, hearing his voice. It was dry and raspy as he spoke into the phone.

"Hi," he clears his throat, "This is Rim Jack and I know this is random but there has been an issue with our house.... And...... I was wondering if my family and I could...um." He stopped, not able to finish the sentence. I couldn't blame him, I wouldn't have gotten that far.

Mom touched his shoulder, "Rim?"

I wanted to take the phone and scream into it, I wanted to rip it from his hands and crush the phone with my own foot. I hated this, I hate every second that we stand here, helpless, homeless, useless, begging for help. I was not that person. I would not expect someone to just let us into their house, baggage and all. We have no other choice, so I bit my lip.

Instead of Dad having to continue, I overheard the other person through the phone who was talking a little too loudly, "Of course you can stay here as long as you like." It sounded like he was more than welcome, but I didn't buy it.

Mom and Dad looked grateful. Dad's lips were even curled into a smile. I risked a glance at Andrew, but he was still burning his eyes into the ground as if he could shoot a laser from his eyes and make a giant hole, he too was biting his lower lip. Was he thinking the same thing I was? Did this hurt him as much as it did me?

"Thanks, we will be on our way now if that's okay?"

The other speaker's voice was again too loud and over welcoming, "That's perfect."

My blood boiled hotter than I thought possible. I shifted my weight as dad took the phone from his ear, uneasy.

"Kids, to the truck,"Mom said. Her voice angered me, she sounded hopeful.

I climbed into my truck and was careful to shut the door, I didn't want to slam it. I had enough things ruined at a time. Before I started the engine Mom stared at me through the window.

"What?"

Without saying anything she pointed her index finger to Dad's truck. I moaned getting out of my vehicle to my feet, "Why can't I take mine?" I asked.

"Andrew needs his and we don't want to crowd their drive way," Dad answered for mom.

Then I wondered who 'their' was. It didn't bother me that I haven't thought of this already. *Were we staying with my grandparents? No. I would have recognized the voice, but why not?*

"Mom, I don't feel like driving," those were the first words from Andrew since he screamed at me, it made me fell guilty, ashamed of myself, as if I set the fire purposely. Ouch, that thought stopped me cold in my tracks, but that's how I felt. Pain refuses to be ignored.

"I will drive your truck then, get into Dad's," she said.

For a moment I didn't move, I was frozen. When Dad honked the horn, I realized that it was for me. I shuffled my feet to the other side and climbed in, my bag hitting me in the back on the way.

Until we got to the end of our long drive way, my eyes were focused out the window. I watched the trees pass by in a warm fuzz of green. We didn't stay at the end long, and I whispered to myself, "Goodbye Jack's Road." Who knew the next time we would be here? If it were up to me, it would be never. I'd have Andrew or Dad come pick up my truck and I would move to Florida, I've been there enough times to know what to expect.

Andrew's phone lit up instantly on the seat beside me. I looked so quickly that all I saw was a blur. I guessed that it was Adoria, Andrew's girlfriend. I don't know what to think about him telling her, but then again why wouldn't he?

We pulled out of the drive way and from that moment on, I could tell that this will be the hardest car ride I've ever had to take.

★★★

I noticed that Dad slowed down and turned the blinker to turn left. I followed Andrew's hand pointing to the house we were apparently staying in, had he been here before? How did he know? This is the first time in history that Andrew is making me question him so much…was it the house? Had that brought him to act differently around me? Or maybe it was just the way I was running back in after my memories I couldn't let go of. Ugh, memories, they were gone, I have none left. Should I make new ones? Should I replace the old ones? I thought back to the bonfires I had with my "friends", or maybe I should just lock these up for safe keeping. As of right now, I'm going to meet the house I will live in for who knows weeks, months? Now for the first time, memories can wait.

The drive way was small, narrow and defiantly not as long. There were already three vehicles parked, as many as I could see. Two were under a roof, and the other was off to the side. The black Dodge was parked sideways and the front was facing toward the house, like it could run it over. Then my eyes trailed to the house itself. From the outside, it was tiny and white. Yes, it had two stories like mine did, but it wasn't quite as big.

There were flowers alongside the sidewalk as we walked quickly in a not so straight line. I really don't know why Mom set the pace so fast, but I didn't want to fall behind.

Once Dad pressed the doorbell, he stood back beside Mom. Then Mom took a backward glance at Andrew and me to see if we were presentable. We were, Andrew was on the right behind Mom and I was on the left, behind Dad. We both held our hands behind our backs and then I looked ahead. I heard Mom whisper for us to smile, but it was too hard.

Nobody came to the door. We stood and stood for what felt like at least fifteen minutes.

"Maybe they aren't home." Mom announced, leaning toward Dad, with a smile on her face.

"No, they would have told us."

Mom didn't say anything after that, she simply nodded and squared her shoulders back to face the door. Then Dad took one step forward and knocked on the door once more.

I thought, *Well, that didn't help anything; we'll still have to stand here for the next two hours before someone will see us.* It was about to rain. I smelled it, surprised that my nose still worked after all the smoke I inhaled today. Tiny, wet droplets started to attack me from above. First it hit my cheek, then my bare arm.

"Hello! Come on in!" I heard a lady speak only to see that someone did come to the door. She looked about five feet, close to the same height as my mom. She had short dark hair and green eyes. Her nose looked long, but her mouth was rather full.

In my peripheral vision, I saw Andrew flash a smile, but my lips declined, I am now homeless, whether someone decides to let me sleep in their room on their bed or not.

Homeless. I thought of that word. It wasn't very pleasant, I didn't like the way it sounded, and to me, I would have never thought this would happen, let alone be called homeless.

"Hello, Rachel," Mom said, in the softest voice imaginable.

I stepped in after Mom and Dad, directly behind Andrew. I closed the door behind me, careful not to slam it and stayed right on Andrew's heels. I smelled vanilla, which made me question what the house looked like, but I couldn't look up, not yet.

Rachel started talking in a voice that was too loud, I didn't understand why. I concentrated on what she was saying, but keep my head down.

"This is the kitchen, please help yourself. Don't worry about asking. This is the dinning room, and that over there is the laundry room. There are two bathrooms downstairs and one upstairs. If you don't mind, the kids can sleep upstairs and we have a basement. I'm sure the girl wouldn't want to spend a night down there, it's cold, but we have blankets." I heard the smile in her voice, but I also could tell she was looking right at me the entire time. Maybe it's because she doesn't know me. I don't know her either.   Why would she stare at a stranger? I consider it rude, but I decided that I would be nice anyway, this is her home and her rules.

"Hello," This was a new voice. It was deeper so I looked up without thinking. It must be her husband, he was much taller, his hair was almost gone but his eyes were a pretty blue.

"May I introduce myself, I don't believe I know some of you," He said. So this was the voice on the phone, completely over-welcoming. I don't know why he said 'some of you', because clearly it was just me. I'm not very social. That doesn't mean I'm shy either, I am just a quiet person, no one understands me and I don't expect them to, so why is there a need to befriend anyone?

Rachel's husband walks up to me as my parents split and Andrew trails off to look around. He sticks a hand out and I take it, "My name is Mathew Hall," he said. I choked up my name before anything else could happen, while I shook his hand.

"My you have pretty eyes," he said. Well, this wasn't scary at all. I am in a complete strangers home, in the place we had to refuge to, and this stranger is telling me I have pretty eyes. This man is so much older than me that it makes it that much more creepy. Instead of turning and bolting for the door to stand in the rain, I swallowed again and spoke, "Thank you," I would have said something along the lines of 'You have a pretty home' but I haven't seen it.

When Mathew turns his back to me and walks back to his wife, I tear my eyes away and begin to look around. I couldn't believe my eyes. Yes, the house was tiny, but on the inside it looks that much more bigger. There were vanilla flowers covering every table top, and a cream color filled the furniture. I saw a stain on their cream colored carpet, but skipped it and continued to look around.

"Shall we head to the upstairs?" Rachel asks, interrupting my own personal tour.

Instead of watching our reactions or waiting for someone to speak, she turned and headed up the long stair case, which also had cream color carpet which is suffocating the steps that I imagine as wood.

I chose the room that overlooked the back yard instead the front. Maybe it would be more peaceful since it is farther away from the road. This is the suburbs, whic I am not use to. I have lived in pure country all my life. This will take some time.

Instead of my floor being cream colored carpet like everything else, it was wood. As frustrating as this all was, I felt more comforted than I ought to be. I usually read before I close in for the night, but reading just didn't feel like the thing to do right now, so I climbed into my small bed and hoped to get some sleep tonight.

Chapter Six

When I wake up in the morning, there are no words to describe how much hatred I feel for myself. I don't know why but it's there. It made me want to turn around and crawl back into the bed that wasn't mine, and just weep. Though weeping wouldn't do anything for me and the longer I stay here, the worse I will feel for not running inside my burning house to steal back my memories. I feel empty and not the kind that makes you jump to conclusions and convince yourself that you're hungry. This feels like I have nothing left. I am nothing. There isn't anything to describe what kind of person I am, there are no memories; there are no clothes that are mine; I have no personality; there are no books.

I frown. I have not but one book to keep as a distraction. I want to try to read as little as possible to make *The Fault In Our Stars* last longer, but the pain is too heavy. I sunk to the floor and stared at the carpet until I realized I have to go to school. The sooner I get there, the sooner this will feel like any other normal day.

When I finally rose to my feet, my eyes were set on the white desk farthest from... not my door, but the bed. It held two outfits of girls clothing. I wondered if Rachel picked it out for me, but I couldn't see it, especially not *two*.

The first was a long plain navy blue shirt, and blue jeans to go with it. If it were mine and it was a normal day, I would have added some ear rings, but this is not mine, and I have no jewelry to wear, besides my charm bracelet.

The next was also a long plain shirt, except it was a light pink, which also went with blue jeans. I sighed and picked up the first outfit, at least the color almost matched my mood, but I guess that color should be black with no hope, but black just didn't seem right. Not because it was too sad, but because it showed no hope, I want to say I had some, but that would be a lie.

The stairs seemed to be longer than ever. I trailed down them feeling half asleep until I got to the kitchen. My eyes almost popped out! So they had a son, and he is cute.

This son of theirs was sitting on the wooden stool which was pushed up to a granite counter and was eating some kind of cereal. I have to admit, this thought never touched the edge of my mind. Maybe this is why I felt the tiniest bit hope rising.

Mom and Dad were also in the kitchen. They looked like they were arguing but when I stepped onto the tile floor, Mom covered her face with her hands and then Dad leaned into mom to whisper something. Maybe I was becoming someone who eavesdrops, because I knew exactly what he said, "Ease up, Embril just walked in," and saw her immediately whip a smile clean onto her face and ask the same question she would have if she didn't leave for work before I got downstairs every morning, "Did you sleep well?"

I had to find a way to not lie, it's not in me, Mom is in a bad place as it is, I did not sleep good, "Yes, last night was fine," it wasn't a total lie, it was finer that I had thought.

Then I remembered this isn't just a normal day and checked the phone that was in my hand. It was seven-ten. Mom should have left for work by now. I opened my mouth to ask why, but thought better of it and clamped my teeth together hoping no one saw my mouth open in the first place.

Instead of asking where the bowls are to fix cereal, I opened the pantry door as if it were my own, with some luck, something different would save me from an awkward breakfast with a stranger.

When I was just about to pull a pop tart from the box, I heard a dish being not so easily sat on the counter to my left. Then a person's voice rang through my ears, "Hope you pick something fast, we're leaving in two minutes." My gut tells me that it was the guy sitting at the counter when I walked in. He was already finished?

Then my thoughts led to something different...what did he mean by *me?*

★★★

This is why I wanted to bring my truck. I knew Andrew would either leave too early every morning or just flat out tell my parents he did not want to drive me to school. He would have before the house caught on fire, but I guess my reaction to my memories startled him more than I thought it had.

The stranger had to drive me to school himself. I was not up for this, I did not ask to use his gas, I gladly would have walked, but since I guess "our" school was further than ten miles from "home", I had to take a vehicle.

Before I could ask his name, not that I was going to, I noticed that he was eyeing my phone every few seconds. What was he doing? Wishing it would float out the window and crush it's own screen so another thing in my life could just disappear? How nice.

"So, do your friends know or do they just not care about um...?" he trailed off his sentence for exactly the reason I knew he was going after. I'm glad he didn't say the actual thing, that would have hurt, he's smart. I like smart.

"Don't have a lot of friends," I stopped thinking that was all I was going to say, but the driver just pursed his lips and that made me think that this could be an opportunity for a friend, I've had many opportunities, but I chose all the wrong paths. Would right now be an appropriate time for a friend? Oh well, that doesn't matter, my goal is to make him feel better.

"I'm more of a reader," I said and held up *The Fault In Our Stars* book I managed to grab before we left.

"What do you do at lunch then?"

His question got me wondering...what DO I do at lunch? Yes, I'm not the typical person who laughs at tables just to get someone to notice me, I have to have something to laugh about, and for that reason, I have no friends. I have my books.

"Read," I say.

43

"Don't you eat?"

I almost throw my head back in laughter, but this stranger might actually become someone I can call a friend, and I'm just not sure if laughing obnoxiously would scare him away or not. So, I bit my lip even though a little giggle slipped through anyway. He must have heard it, because he laughed a lot louder than I did, I guess he was comfortable with me already, or just a risk taker. Perhaps I was wrong. Maybe laughing loudly wouldn't have scared him away, maybe it would draw him in, like it did me.

"Yes," I said once we finished laughing.

"Good wouldn't want you to starve."

I didn't say anything else. I could have nodded, but his eyes were constantly focused on the road, I didn't want to distract him. Later in the drive to school, I thought it was too quiet so I was going to ask of his name, but I couldn't seem to get it past my teeth.

First block was completely annoying, tiring, and boring. The entire class was just so obnoxious that Mr. Tidewalk couldn't get them to calm down. I watched as the words he said fell off his lips in an angry manner, he looked like a cow trying to chew a thick piece of grass, his lips came together so hard after every word that they bounced back. This was terrifying. I should look away, but something in his anger made mewant to laugh. The entire block went this way for the entire hour and a half. Sometimes the students would shut up for two minutes and let our teacher recover himself, and when he would start to teach, then the situation flooded over and got worse.

As of right now, Mr. Tidewalk is leaning against his desk with one hand pressed to his forehead. With each episode and after the class settles, it takes longer and longer for him to recover. I wonder if he has had either (one) anger issues, or (two) has trouble hiding his feelings. Perhaps I should bring him some chill pills because he looks like he is about to explode and honestly, I don't want to be in the room when that happens.

Then I heard a few mumbles behind me.

"The teacher looks stressed out."

"Yeah, I think that's the goal," someone with a deep voice commented.

The girl with the light voice replied with more curiosity, "Why?"

"So we don't have to do work," someone else said from across the room. Then it happened again, the classroom went crazy. I understand they don't want to do work. I of all people do not want to work, but it takes my mind off the bad things and this certainly isn't doing any good except to give me a headache.

I glance at Michel beside me, he isn't enjoying this either, but he isn't doing anything to stop it. He keeps staring down into a book like he is having trouble concentrating, I wonder why he isn't doing anything, I'd think he would be the one in the middle of it all because he is so popular, but maybe I'm mis-reading him. What makes Michel Shrew one of the popular kids?

I didn't want to do this. I am not good at making friends, but I want to go home and the only way to get that guy from the "friend house" to be on my side, I need to convince him I can make friends on my own, no matter how hard that seems. This should be easy. I've talked to Michel before, so I swallowed hard, noting that my throat is so dry it hurts, but I talk, "Hey, why don't you try and stop this disaster?" I have to lean over so he could hear me.

For a second he scares me because he looks in my direction and says nothing. Did I do something wrong; something un-cool? Will he go about and spread ridiculous rumors about me? or worse, tell as many people as he can to not talk to me?

Instead of scaring me more, he just smiles and says, "Why aren't you?"

I almost laugh and answer with an edge to my voice that I didn't want to. "Good point."

Michel just stares at me. I stare back wishing he would say something. Its been so long I can feel sweat on my forehead and my face is getting hot, but when I take my eyes off Michel for an inch of a second, the clock behind him tells me it's only been a few seconds. Not even a minute. So I look away, and we didn't speak for the rest of the class.

Second block was the exact opposite. I sat in my seat and took notes like everyone else. It was so quiet I thought maybe it would take my headache away, but it got worse.

Lunch. I had it packed and my table picked out as always. I felt like I should be expecting something different to happen, but I shake it off and sit down with my book. Before I can finish the first sentence, I feel the presence of some other human being at my table. No one sits here, no one notices, I have no friends just my books, who could it possibly be?

I look up to see the guy who drove me to school this morning sitting there.

"Hey, there," he says just before biting into an apple. I didn't respond.

"What book is that?" he tries to talk with a full mouth, it's disgusting but I don't look away, "Stuff you wouldn't like," I said, without yelling. He was frustrating me, and I don't know how.

For a few seconds, its quiet and I go back to my book. Just as I expected, I got interrupted again, this time halfway through my chapter, so I gave up reading and started to eat, not answering my company's questions.

"I don't understand why you are ignoring me, I'm trying to be you're friend," the guy is now sitting inches from me instead of across the table. This way, it is impossible to not say *something*. He knows I can hear him.

"Why do you assume I want friends?" I asked. *(which I do, but not like this... not out of pity)*.

"'Cause you look lonely and everyone wants friends."

"Fine."

Then I see heads pop up around me. Everyone is staring at the girl who randomly just got one friend. A male with blond hair leans closer to me than I would like, and whispers, "How did you manage to get yourself a friend, and Cameron of all people?" He laughs as he throws himself back into his chair. Did he just make fun of me? My first instinct was to throw something back at him, but I have no words, I don't even know him. So Cameron was his name, the person I am now living with.

I stuff my food back into my lunch box and open my book again, this time I'm only pretending to read, but the people don't look away. They stare at me for at least eight minutes before I get up and walk to the bathroom. Eating lunch in the stall is just gross, and if they randomly fill up, I'd feel guilty for not giving it to someone. Besides, worse things could happen in the bathroom. So I stare at myself in the mirror until the fourth block bell rang, trying to figure out why those people had to be so mean. What were they looking at?!

★★★

The car ride back from school was silent. There were few words between us,but Cameron actually addressed to me that he didn't know my name. It came out like a demand, "So, now you know my name....what is yours?"

Part of me wanted to ignore him for asking a stupid question because it seemed to me like he never wanted me to know his name, like it meant something bad, but it was not a stupid question like it seemed to be.

"Embril."

Cameron nodded and that was the last conversation we had.

The house looked different, not in any serious change but it felt different. I've been apart from it for eight hours and coming back made it feel more cozy than I ever would want it to. What's going to happen if I get too attached? What if we never move out? No, I will move out when I'm old enough to, and I'm pretty close, technically speaking, Andrew is already able, by the way he acts, he pays his insurance and gas money, the only thing I can't see him doing, is his laundry.

I went upstairs and my room didn't feel like the rest of the house, it still felt taken, instead of me borrowing it. I climbed into bed and shut off the lamp. It

was too dark to see anything, so I slid further into the
covers and closed my eyes.

Chapter Seven

The next day was normal. Teachers taught, students listened, others acted chaotic and lunch with Cameron was silent. No one stared at me again, except the one dude who laughed at me for talking to Cameron, he only stared at me, his dark eyes burning into mine, but I didn't look away until he did. (Score one)

The rest of the week flew by. The hours were spread apart into inches moving forward like a time bomb, but a fast one. Friday night, after I got home from school, I was excited that I didn't have to go back to that wretched place until Monday, but I didn't want to be here at this house either, so I headed up the stairs, slumping my shoulders. This room still felt odd, like it was twisted and I still feel like a thief. I don't want to be in here. Instead of sobbing on my own, I went to Andrew's room, but he fell asleep, in full clothing. What was I going to do? Mom and Dad are probably busy and I just don't know the owners well enough to talk to them and I don't want to.

I spotted Cameron's room down the hall from Andrew's, I walked as quietly as I could to sneak in there and see what he was doing. When I looked, there was no sign of him, but I never thought so much character could be put into one room, there were many drawings posted to the wall. Was he an artist? Cameron had two long book cases on the side of his room, right under his window. Does he like to read like me? Then lastly, was a T.V. It was pulled up to a music station, I got closer to read the song because it was playing so quietly I never would have heard it if I hadn't seen the title with my own eyes. It was country. Was his dream to be a country star or a composer?

In this tiny cavern of a room, I see so many possibilities, so many different people, built up inside one person, I love that. Then my thoughts surprised me, *what if he saw me in here? What would I say? Could I lie?* I put one foot in front of the other, pumping my arms.

Cameron wasn't in the hall way, so I was clear. I let out a huge sigh and walked normal to the room I had stolen, looking at the ground.

When I bumped the door on my way in, I heard a gasp so I looked up immediately, my heart racing. It was just Cameron. I know who it is, so why is my heart still sprinting? Hurry up and get to the finish line, I growl inside my head, but my heart just would not listen.

"You okay?" Cameron asked. Probably because I stood there too long, with my hand over my chest.

I swallowed, "Yeah, well, no, but yes, I mean you scared me but I'm okay, but I'm not okay." That was terrible. Did he understand what I meant? I opened my mouth to explain it better, but he sat down on the foot of the bed and patted the spot next to him.

Letting my right hand fall, I walked to the spot next to Cameron and whispered again, "I am not okay." That time, my eyes got wet. I can not cry, not in front of Cameron; not in front of my only friend right now, or ever. I cannot. I will be strong. I will be brave.

I choked the threatening tears back and my eyes sting, I will *not* loose it.

"You can tell me," he said.

I started to shake my head no, but that's just not me, and I can't lie right now. I can barely speak.

Breathe in, breathe out.

"Okay," I sniffle, "I have been trying so hard to fit in now, to be alright and just live life, that I don't know the reason I am not happy. Not until tonight. Tonight I went to your room to see if you were there, and I saw all the drawings and books. I saw so many possibilities of the future and so many memories of the past," I wrap my hand around my other wrist and suffocate it, I will *not* loose it, "It reminded me of my burnt up memories, my house lost those memories so I did too, and now I have nothing." I flinched at the words 'burnt up'.

A tear slid down my cheek, *thanks for listening.* Cameron didn't say anything. He just takes my hand and holds it. My heart speeds up again and I can't breathe, but I think anyway. All those books I read, there is no record.   All those pages ripped from the story, all the words, now mean nothing.   Every childish toy I had, turned into ash, Every cook book we ever owned, every fork we ate with and every spoon we licked the icing off of. It's all gone.

Another tear escapes, *stop it.*

"It's all gone," I said one more time and I pulled my hand away.

Cameron gets up like he's about to walk out without a word, like he's heard enough and can't take it. His back is staring me in the face, so I put my head in my hands and bend over to my knees, why did this happen to *me?*

Instead of walking out, Cameron turns back to face me and I lift my head to see him smile.

"You need a distraction," he says.

"I have one, its just almost over," I replied tilting my head to my book on the nightstand.

"No, you need to have fun," he says walking back toward me.

"Reading *is* fun," I sniffle again.

"Yes, but lots of fun," he stops and I have to ask myself why, but he shows no sign and continues, "Why don't you go kayaking with us?"

"Kayaking? Not a good idea I'm not---

Cameron cuts me off, "Don't say coordinated," he made my brain stop working, he seriously just read my mind, how is that possible?

"How did you know-

"I see you in the morning, reaching for a pop tart, it isn't as graceful as you think it is." He cuts me off again and I laugh. This is perfect, right now, he is my perfect friend, I've never had one of those, and right now I want to be exactly like him.

"I think Andrew wants to come," I said, choosing my words carefully, 'come' means I am going, as though 'go' would have been saying 'take him instead'.

Cameron is now standing back to his spot when I first came in, so close to the bed he could reach down and touch it, but he doesn't sit and he looks down at me to make sure I can see his crooked smile. "Lets go ask him," he says yanking me off the bed, which makes me laugh again. I can not believe how he distracted me so easily, I don't know how to handle this. He made me laugh more than I cried, or was it just his presence, or myself? Did I somehow manipulate my emotions so that one could be stronger than the other? Is that even possible? I don't know, but I don't care about finding out.

"You go, tell me in the morning," I yawn, "I am-

"Sleepy?" he asks.

I yawn again, covering my mouth same as before, "You are a mind reader," I said and smiled just a little.

I noticed that Cameron is still holding my hand from when he yanked me off the bed, my feet flush to my ears and he let go then said, "Okay."

Once Cameron left, I shut the door and slid into bed. Instead of crying, screaming, or laughing again, I smiled and I pretended. I slept with a good feeling all night.

★★★

Saturday morning I woke to the sound of a knock on my door.

"What?" I yelled.

It's Saturday. I find the feeling of not wanting to get up inside me, but the knocking continues. Ugh. Finally, I got up and walked to the door. "What?" I asked again, but this time I really opened my eyes.

Cameron is standing in my door way, and I'm still in the tank top and shorts I slept in, there's no telling how bad my hair looks. Then again, why do I care?

"Time for kayaking," he says as he bounces on his feet.

"At three in the morning?"

"Yep," Cameron says and stumbles as he walked backward from me. That made me laugh. Hmm.

When I pick up my phone, it doesn't say three a.m. like it feels. It is eight o' clock. Then I look through the empty closet, I have nothing to wear for kayaking. All I have are the jeans and shirts that Rachel sat on my desk every few days for school, but kayaking? I look In the

mirror, I do look disgusting.   Perfect. The good news is
that it can be fixed. I tugged and pulled on my tank top
and shorts, then threw my hair into a pony tail awhile
racing down the stairs.

"Mom?"

"Yes?"

"I have nothing to wear."

"Oh, um. Rachel?" She calls to one of the owners
of the place we are living in and asked if there was
something I could wear. I already don't like this.

"Oh yes! I forgot, there is something on the
couch!" I overheard. Or perhaps Rachel was still using
her loud voice, I have no idea why.

Mom points to the couch in the living room and
then trailed to the kitchen, probably for coffee.

Walking to the edge of the couch I searched for
clothing. There was a two piece swim suit, folded up. I
picked it up and saw that it had many colors. I think it's
a little too colorful and I didn't want to wear it, but I had
no other choice, so I grabbed the cover-up and ran
upstairs to change.

★★★

I left my hair like it was. That was a mistake.
Little strands of hair are falling out and they land right
into the spaces I wish they wouldn't.

We are already on the water. My kayak is red, and
the paddle is black and white. I have kayaked before, in
our tiny pond because I wanted to try it when I was very
young. My parents said......what did they say? I can't
remember....have I truly lost all memories? I should not
try to think back. Anyway, I should not have part of that
memory. It should not exist.

We hadn't been out long, we had only just got
everyone into the water and we had started traveling in
two lines. Mom and Dad did not come with us, so it was
just Cameron, Andrew, Rachel, Mathew and myself.
Rachel and Mathew were up front, then Andrew and
Cameron in the middle. I am last. How did this happen,
I was first into the water!

"Hey, someone wait up!" I shouted, but everyone pretended to not hear me, or maybe I really was too far away. Panic flooded in and stabbed my insides.

Don't leave me, don't leave me, don't leave me!

Something in me tells me to be a coward and yell for help... something along the lines of, "Help I am just drowning here!" I don't want to drown, but I don't want them to have the panicky feeling I am experiencing now. I paddled faster but couldn't catch up to them. Why won't they stop and look for me? Don't they know I'm not *up there, with them?*

The current slowed and I saw that a tree had fallen into the water. I felt sad for the tree. When did that happen? Did it get attacked the same time I did?

Then when I got closer to the fallen tree, I came out of my trance and realized that I was headed straight for it. I started to paddle... hard! Nothing happened. Is this just a dream, a dream about kayaking tomorrow and this really isn't Saturday yet? *When I get caught on the tree I will wake up and everything will be okay, I will not drown.* Something in my head tells me that this isn't a dream, and I stop paddling for a second to pinch myself to make sure. Ouch! Yep, I'm sure. I don't know what will happen when I hit that small little baby tree. It was so full of life and had a future, just like my house did, like the thing called memories did. I wiped at my eyes and told myself to think straight. What should I do?

"Hey! Hey guys, what do I do?" I shouted.

"Hey! Is anyone listening to me?" I shouted again but no one answered. They are around the bend, so I can't see them.

I kept shouting and getting zero answers. I tried to think of a different strategy and shout at the same time, but it didn't work, I just kept paddling. When I got closer, I noticed that the current was pulling me in toward the tree. I screamed and that time I think someone heard me, but it was too late. They are too late to save me. I am too late to save myself. The tip of my kayak hit the tree and then the left side... I flipped!

Thankfully I gasped for air just in time, but started letting go of my bubbles too fast. I am started to run out of air. I tried to kick myself up, searching for oxygen but couldn't find any! I kicked harder and harder, my head hitting the top of the kayak each time. *I am under the water and my own kayak is drowning me, I am drowning!* My lungs burn like fire each time I gulp in water, it hurts and the water flows in too easily. Another attack? On me? Why? I kicked one more time and my head hit the kayak again. My head began to throb, my eyes and throat were stinging, my legs were tired. I tried not to give up, but my legs wouldn't move, and I sunk.

"Em! Embril! Where did she go? Embril we're here can you come up? Try to swim up!"

It was Andrew's voice. *I can not do this to him again, I have to fight for him.* Suddenly I saw a figure swimming toward me. It's Andrew! *I want to kick, but I have no air, I have no energy.*

"Your parents need you, don't leave them!" The next voice was not Mathew's, nor Rachel's, it belonged to Cameron. Though his plead was clear, to me it sounded like don't leave *me.* Why would I want to? Why would I want to leave him or Andrew, my parents or even Cameron's parents after they have been so nice to my family? The coward voice in my head told me to give up and just fall, but I don't want to be a coward. *I will not leave them!* So, I fight it with all I have, then Andrew grabbed my arm, but we go nowhere. My leg was stuck. Something was wrapped around my ankle and was keeping me under the water. When I reach down to pull it off, it felt like a weed or moss.

I'm scared.

I will be brave!

I used all my strength, the little that I have physically, and yanked it from my ankle while ripping it into shreds, just as Andrew pulled me up.

My vision goes black at the edges and I don't think I am breathing.

Give up.

Don't give up.

It's silent. The world goes dark. I finally cough, the water spilling out of my lungs. It won't stop. The water just keeps coming. I turned my head to the side as more water flowed out. It hurts more but comes out just as easily as it went in. I'm jealous. The water does as it wants without effort.

I raise up to my knees and cough, "I'm sorry." Salty tears strike my face, why do I cry so much?

"For what? Don't be," Cameron growls like I'm being ridiculous, but he wasn't the one I was apologizing to.

Andrew looks up at me, "Of course, this isn't the first."

Andrew is angry with me, but this incident, I had no control over, he must forgive me *this* time. Then I wondered how bad this was for him. Not having to save my life twice, within almost a week of torture for me, but the house situation. Andrew lived there too, his things are destroyed too. My brother was attacked too. His senior year in high school, and this happens to him of all people?

I have to admit, now is the first time I want to take a trip to the moon, and never come back. Maybe there is something up there that I need, something like me.

Everyone climbed back into their kayaks, and for a moment, I don't. Rachel and Mathew finally talk, both at the same time, "Its, okay."

I nod and climb in. Cameron's parents go first again, to lead the way, Andrew takes up the middle, and Cameron stays in the back by me. How much experience does he have?

We don't talk. That is for another day. Cameron stays close to me until It's over. Some of the time I think he was about to reach for my hand, like his parents did after I flipped, in a friendly way; but he never fully did.

I wonder why he asked me not to specifically leave *him*. But maybe that's not what he meant, so I keep paddling until we reach the end.

Chapter Eight

The sun shines through the window and it hurts my eyes. I'm in this tiny room that I'm borrowing and I have my book in front of me. It's almost finished, right after the big plot twist. Today is supposed to be a lazy day, and I feel so exhausted from being attacked again yesterday.

"Hey," I look up to see Cameron coming in with a muffin, "What some breakfast?" he asks.

I sit still for a minute, "No, I'm not hungry, no thanks, though."

"Hey are you okay? You look...", He doesn't finish his sentence but I feel sick.

"Yeah I'm fine."

"Liar," Cameron said, and walked back out the door.

I didn't appreciate that. Wouldn't I know if I wasn't okay?

Mom comes in next, "Oh my," she says hesitating to come in, then she knocks on the door and I nod.

"Want to go shopping?"

"I don't like shopping."

"Oh, yes you do, now stop being pathetic and lets go."

Mom stands there and waits until I decide to get to my feet. I don't want to go, but this closet is empty, and I need something more my style.

Mom and I drive to Tullahoma, a place that isn't too far away, but it isn't exactly close either. The first store we go into is called Bargain-mart. My least favorite place for clothing, but it's the cheapest, so I walk through the parking lot with my mom on my side and the doors open for us.

We walk to the clothes and look around. I put two pairs of leggings in our buggy and tell mom that I'm going to the bathroom. When I'm on my way back, I found myself in the book section. *The Fault In Our Stars* is almost over and I need something new. I picked up a book with a hard cover. Then I put it back down because it had a mark on it, the mark looked to be like someone got mad and drew all over the price sticker with a red marker, some of it got onto the cover.

"You like books?"

Instead of answering, I turn and run. If it were a normal person to talk to me back there, I would have answered, but this was the same guy with brown hair and brown eyes that has been stalking me…*what did he want?*

I expected him to follow me, or to at least see him again, but I didn't.

The next place we went to was called Rue 58. This is actually one of my favorites. The perfume they sell smells so good and the clothes…it's the perfect design for me.

Mom gasped, so I followed her gaze. To my right there was a sign that announced a sale, each shirt was only four dollars. I didn't see any jeans or skirts, only shirts. I picked up one that has a chevron pattern on the back and got Mom's attention. "This one?"

"If you like it and it's four dollars, help yourself."

I walked along the rack examining shirts, I put back the ones I don't like or that I wouldn't wear, and draped the others over my arm.

When we reached the "friend house" again, it felt that it took forever to get all the bags of clothes inside. Instead of taking them all to my room immediately, we just put them in the kitchen floor so I could go get the other bags quicker.

Finally, we finished and mom reversed Dad's car back to it's usual borrowed spot.

"Everyone, I have an announcement," Rachel said clasping her hands.

"We do this every year," Cameron said and headed upstairs instead of waiting for the news that I guess he already knows.

"What's going on?" Mom said when she got back inside, closing the door too quietly. Andrew, Dad, and me were sitting on the couch, Mathew in his chair and Rachel was standing up ready to talk. So Mom took the other chair, across from Mathew.

"Yes. Every year, our family comes to our house around this time for a sort of reunion party," Rachel continued without letting my Mom stop her little-big announcement, "They will be here tomorrow."

The room dispersed. Andrew sighed and went upstairs, Dad went outside with Mathew and I took my bags upstairs, with my Mom's help.

★★★

Here it is, Monday again. I'm wearing some of the clothes that I bought yesterday and the family is in the kitchen, eating breakfast. Rachel cooked potatoes, sausage, eggs, and bacon this morning. I was the last person down. Big breakfasts aren't really my thing, so I take a plate and get only potatoes, then sit next to Cameron.

We ate in silence. Though Andrew is a loud chewer, I could hear his teeth clamping into everything, and the gulp of his throat when he took a drink.

Cameron walked out the door first, "We're leaving!" he called, and I followed him out.

"You need friends," says Cameron.

"Um, no thanks, I'm fine."

"No you are not, stop it! Embril, you are lying to yourself and everyone else gets caught up in it. You are not okay, I can see it right through you, I think you need a distraction other than...books!" he is shouting at me from the other side of his truck.

My head gets hot and I'm afraid I'm going to burst into flames and burn something of his too. Instead, I answer in the same shouting tone, "I know who I am, and I don't need friends to help me get by in life. Yes it is nice, and I like having you around, but I am just as okay without friends! They just hurt you all the way around, and it hurts me that you think I can't move on without someone right beside me!"

Ugh, I am mad. I want to make him feel the pain I'm in. I am not depressed, even though it feels that way, I don't need help or therapy, I am almost normal, I don't care if I'm old one day and wish I did things differently....I don't need friends.

Cameron gets in and doesn't tell me to do anything, I could walk away...but school is a distraction. So, I hit him where it hurts, I get in too, but I slam the door of his beautiful truck.

"Careful," he says, eyeing me, "We are going off on a friend spree, I know you don't need friends and I'm...fine, I'm sorry. You might like having friends, really you never know, so we're going to start with my cousin, Dustin."

I roll my eyes, but my mouth stays shut. I know he said sorry, but that doesn't make what he said hurt any less. He doesn't know. Cameron does not know the pain I am in, he does not know what it's like to lose everything you own.

"Cameron," I just had a brilliant idea.

"What?"

"Do you, I mean, I forgive you," I need to take the other route, make it easier for him to say yes.

"Good."

"Do you want to go house shopping with me?"

"House shopping?"

"Yeah, so I can try to get my parents to believe I'm ready for a new one," it's a long shot I know, so I turn my head to the road and squeeze my eyes shut because I don't want to see Cameron's reaction to what I just said.

"Don't you think its still a little early for that? And besides, that's your parents job," he says.

I just want to be out of here, I don't like sharing a house that isn't mine with strangers, and I want my own things, I want my life back...I want my library. My library is never coming back though. I sigh. I wish it would.

"Yeah, but they have had a hard time too, I want to make it easier for them."

"Okay, I will, but you have to follow up on my friend spree."

Why didn't I see this coming? I look down at my hands, but in my peripheral vision I see Cameron smile just a little bit. Why?

"Okay, I'm in."

Cameron parks in the usual parking spot. When I get out, I see a completely different school.

"*What happened?*"

"Beats me," Cameron responds and without hesitation, he walks away from me, from his truck, locking it into place. How could he just walk away without any more surprise to his voice? Maybe I missed something, or maybe I've been too much into books and my own life than everything else and my school was always like this...I am selfish.

Then I looked around, there was a girl with bright green hair which transformed to bright yellow, she had a pair of scissors in her hand. I watched as the girl clipped off her own hair, did she mean to make it uneven? I looked to my left and saw two trucks racing down the road, in my direction, one red and the other black, but just like it.

"Hey loner, did Cameron *leave?*" The guy driving the red truck was actually talking to me, I'm actually associating, well not yet.

"Yeah, Cameron is the worst for that, see you loner," the guy driving the black truck was nicer, but he looked familiar. I glanced back at the red truck driver, the color reminded me of my truck, but I pushed that to the side. The guy in the red truck was the same guy who's been making fun of me, I look back to guy driving the black truck and he looked a lot like red truck guy...are they brothers?

When they passed, I saw names in a sticker like form on the back windshield, both of them. The red truck drivers said, 'Tyler' and in all lower case letters in the bottom right hand corner, it read, 'Einstein'. So red truck driver/bully's name was Tyler Einstein. I realized the black truck was the same way, but it was a different name, 'Tanner' 'Einstein', they *are* brothers.

The rest of the day flew by. It went too fast, I don't remember anything my teachers tried to teach me, and I certainly don't remember anything else. It was a normal day. I just don't have my own house to come back to.

My heart falls, it becomes blue with tears, though I am not crying. I feel broken, and like the pieces sailed to Europe but others flew to Paris, there is no returning.

★★★

It's chaotic. At the 'friend house' everyone is scrambling everywhere, picking up things they threw down days ago, fetching things someone else tells them to get and stuffs the untouchable things in the garage.

"What? What do I do with this?" I try to yell to Rachel over the hum of the vacuum. I have no idea where to put the dusting rag I just used, but Rachel turned to Mathew to discuss something with him. I searched and found the laundry room, and tossed it in the wash without pushing the start button.

Finally, things calm down, the vacuum dies and everyone ends up in the living room. It takes me awhile to realize that I'm intensely staring at the door... who will come in, anyone I know already, someone I don't want to meet, any of my old friends? But then I remembered that this is their family. The chance of seeing anyone I know is highly impossible. My shoulders shrug and I relax a little, just until the first doorbell rings. Suddenly I'm nervous again. Maybe I would see my younger self. Then I flinch, that's not possible...where did that thought even come from?

Rachel opens the door squealing at the top of her lungs which makes my ears hurt so I cover them up.

"Embril," my Mom says, and gives me a dirty look, so I take them down and push them to my sides.

Rachel sequels again.

The couple finally made their way to me. The first arrivers are young, they look to be like they just got married.

"Hi, I'm Gali nice to meet you," the girl stretched out her hand toward me, and I took it. My eyes instantly tore off to her husband. I sure hope that's him. I hope this is Dustin, like Cameron said my new friend would be, I want him to see that I am already almost there.

"This is-

The man cuts Gali off, "I'm Curt," he said.

62

Great.

It's not *him.*

"Hi Curt," I said making sure to pronounce the 't' like he did, very clearly.

In the background I see Cameron, he sticks his right hand out the door, his smile is as wide as it can go, and I find myself smiling because it's pretty. I like his smile.

That must be Dustin, but I can't see him yet, he is on the other side of the door. I shake my head and return my eyes back to Curt, but he is gone and there stands Gali.

"Forgive my husband, he gets impatient," she smiles at me.

"Oh, it's okay, I got distracted, who are you to...um?" I didn't know who to ask of so my words stopped and Gali laughs at me, "I'm Rachel's niece."

"Okay."

"I'm going to find Curt, see you around," she says a little too jumpy. Then I wonder why they didn't ask about me, they have never met me and I'm defiantly not related. Maybe Rachel already told them all that they have visitors, I don't know.

I shift my weight to my left foot, eager to see who Dustin is. When he steps out of the door way and I can fully see him, my heart stops. All of the sudden my chest hurts and my throat is squeezing together. I should move, I should run and find my way to a park or just outside, *away.* My feet stay planted and I can not tear my eyes apart from the brown hair and brown eyes that has attacked me before. It's *him,* and he is standing right here in *this* house!

"Come, there is someone I want you to meet," Cameron says and starts to walk toward me.

No, no, no, no, no.

I tune Cameron out, I tune everyone out, all I hear is the silent ring in my ears, I can hear my heartbeat too.

Go away, I tell him, *get away from me.*

The words stick in my head, they never come through my teeth, so Dustin is still here, right in front of me. That is when it hits me, am I afraid of him? I guess that I am afraid of this person who attacked me, and now I know why. Dustin is my attacker, he burnt down my house, and he flipped my kayak. Dustin is a monster. This is my one time to be brave, but I am not brave; no matter how much I wish that I was, I am just not.

Ice falls down my face. Never mind, it is a cold tear, and it hurts, it feels like needles, a thousand needles in one place.

"Embril? Hey, wake up, this is," *don't say his name,* "Dustin."

I imagine myself screaming but I pull it together, Cameron has seen me fall apart too many times, he needs to see I am strong and okay, he must think that I can get along with Dustin.

So I take a deep breathe and try to make it seem unnoticeable even though I think I failed, and go on, "Hi," I stick out my hand.

"Dustin takes it and shakes, his cold skin flashes me back to when he took my arm in the store, I close my eyes.

"Embril are you okay?"

This time it wasn't Cameron. It was Dustin who was asking, so I responded too quickly, "Yes, I'm fine."

I pulled my hand away as fast as possible and pushed it into my pocket, maybe this way Cameron wouldn't see my hand shake.

Chapter Nine

The reunion is not over yet. Cameron and Dustin are in the living room talking to someone I don't know yet.   I sat in the kitchen waiting for them to come back like Cameron said they would.   Instead, I freeze up because I see Dustin walking to me—without Cameron—I take a sip of lemonade and then ball my right hand up into a fist.

"Hello," Dustin says.

I almost choke, "If you *ever* attack me again you will find yourself locked in a basement with no water." My nails were digging into my palms. "Don't think about us actually being friends." My hand hurts- "I know what you did."

Dustin throws his hands up to protect himself, and opens his mouth, "Shut up," I said and stormed over to Cameron, unclenching my hand.

"Hey!" Cameron says almost too happy.

"Hello," I respond and wish my voice didn't sound so irritated.

"What did Dustin say?"

Oh no, should I lie? Should I tell Cameron that Dustin and I hit it off great and are good friends now so Cameron can stop this insane friend-spree? Maybe that's too harsh, or too much so it would seem like I'm exaggerating? Would I be able to come up with a real enough story and hope that Dustin will play along?

There is another possibility, I could tell the truth. I could tell Cameron that Dustin didn't say anything, that he just stood next to me. Perhaps I don't have to tell Cameron that I almost exploded and threatened him with the stupidest but only thing I could think of.

I chose the truth option, but not the whole truth, "Nothing, he just stood next to me," I rapidly bring my hand up to my mouth and bit off the tips of my fingernails, I hope he believes me.

"Oh, okay," Cameron frowns. So he does believe me, but I don't like to see him upset, though lying could throw me off hand, the situation could become worse.

"Is that a bad thing?"

"Well, I was just hoping ya'll would talk or something," he says looking straight over to Dustin who is drinking lemonade by the counter I just left.

"I'm sorry."

"Don't worry about it, I will talk to him."

Please no, I don't want Cameron trying to get Dustin to talk to me about something, *anything,* does Dustin have enough courage to lie to his cousin?

"You don't have to," I almost spit the words at him, I didn't mean for it to sound mean or rude. What Cameron wants to do is the last thing I want, but at the same time I want Cameron to be happy, it's just my instinct.

"I'm going to," this time Cameron isn't as jumpy when he talks, he sounds more mad at me, I don't like this either.

"Seriously, Cam," I half jog after him as he walks in Dustin's direction.

Then Cameron grabs my wrist to still me, "Don't call me Cam, I'm doing you a favor, stay here." He lets my wrist go to stare at me for about ten seconds. It felt like forever, but I kept my eyes locked on his.

When he got two feet from Dustin, I could not do it, I could not stand there and wait to instantly become friends with a person who has the intention to attack me over and over, I will not let *my* attacker get what he wants, he has destroyed my life.

I ran.

★★★

My room feels cold. My room is never cold, possibly, it's just me. I run to my bed and roll into my covers in a shape like a crescent. My eyes dart to the door as Cameron slips in.

My thoughts tell me to turn to my stomach, but that might give the impression to Cameron that I don't want to talk to him, otherwise I would.

My eyes are closed, but that doesn't stop me from feeling the bed sink at my feet.

"I'm-

"Don't apologize," Cameron interrupts me. I close my eyes again and sit up to lean against the bed frame.

"Just answer this question and I will forgive you," he stops, and I can feel that he never looked at me, "What is going on? Why are you being so...so?"

I open my eyes, Cameron shakes his head but keeps his eyes focused on the floor. I can't answer his question, I can't tell him what I threatened to do, I can not tell him about what Dustin did. How would he react? I don't think I can bear seeing Cameron, yell at me.

Then he finally looks at me, "Well?"

I'm looking at him too, Cameron's eyes are glossy blue, as if they would break if I told him the truth, but I can't lie, I wasn't completely born with that ability.

I kept my mouth shut, and felt my eyes gloss up too, then I look away.

Cameron gets up and prodded to the door.

"Cameron?" I ask.

He stops with his right hand on the knob, "Will you stay?" I'm not asking him to stay the entire night, I just want to talk about normal things until I'm sure he has forgiven me.

Cameron doesn't say anything, he doesn't even make a sound, except to close the door.

Chapter Ten

Today is Sunday. When I woke up, my phone read eight o' clock. I went to my closet and suddenly wished to be out of this borrowed home, this borrowed room. I saw that part of the wall was painted a dark green color, and the upper half was painted orange. The rest of the room was painted light blue, but the sight of the closet filled me with disgust.

Then I took my fingers, glancing at my bitten off nails, and searched through my closet for anything to wear. After a few minutes, I found nothing. I let my arms fall and my head fell with them. My eyes floated around the floor and back up to my clothes, but on the way back up, I saw a colorful drawing right next to the baseboard. I bent down to see it better. It happened to be a tiny drawing of a house... on the wall. *How ironic.* The tiny house has a front yard, and there is dog and a boy. Then an idea pops into my head. I'm going house shopping!

"Mom, can I take the truck?"

"Sure!"

This surprised me. She didn't even ask where I was going.

I chose to wear blue jeans that roll up from my ankle, a black shirt with sleeves that come to my elbows, and shoes that cover my toes.

Dad's truck is red. It's a Dodge and it's big, almost too big for me to see out the windshield, but it will suffice.

First, I went to the store and picked up one of those papers that advertise houses for sale . I've never looked at one, since my family and I always planned on staying in that one house. My eyes tear up, so I shook my head and focused on the paper.

When I walked out of the store, it felt cooler than it did when I walked in. Just as I got to the truck, tiny water droplets start to prickle at my skin, like something was trying to eat me alive, like a bird would a dead body.

It felt like I would have been eaten, if those memories were saved by me, in *my* house.

I rushed to open the door and slide myself inside before the seat got wet. Part of me wanted to go back, and continue this trip on another day. Then the other side of me doesn't want to go back, because that shelter is a borrowed home, a borrowed room, with borrowed possessions and there is no point in making memories there.

I stuck the key into the ignition and backed out of the parking space. The droplets of water fell one by one onto the glass around me. The rain builds up, each droplet growing until the space is full, and the top overflows.

As I'm driving down the road, the rain got so hard that I couldn't see. I was afraid that I might drive off the side of the road, but I kept my hope and trusted my hands on the steering wheel, and the person who taught me to drive... Andrew.

I wish he would forgive me already, I didn't mean to hurt him the way I did. I was thinking about me and my possessions. I was selfish. Maybe I still am.

I came up to the first house. The driveway was paved.

I parked close enough to the house that I didn't need to see the inside. The window seals were painted an ugly yellow, which could be fixed, but my Dad wouldn't continue with this house, so neither would I.

The next house looks gorgeous. It looks nothing like the picture in the paper I'm holding. There is a single door with a designed window, the house is made out of brick –like our old one- and you can see the second story from outside.

I felt myself cringe at the thought of saying our 'old' house, but that's exactly what it is now.

I take the key and fit it into my pocket just before walking up to the house.

The front porch isn't as big as I would like it to be, but the outside view is perfect.

The driveway is a full mile. The gravel looks like it was just put into place, some holes covered up.

I forget the drive way for a second to knock on the door, and the driveway creeps back to my mind as I'm waiting for the sellers to let me into their home.

★★★

The last house was smaller than I had expected. The porch was just the right size but the drive way was so short you could still see the road. I'm not a fan of roads, I'm still getting use to the suburbs house I am temporarily living in. The inside was better, but worse. The walls were a cream color, which looked nice, but easy to get dirty. Then there were only two bed rooms, meaning I would have to share with Andrew, or sleep on the couch because I know I would loose that bet.

The two bed rooms, stopped me. No way was I looking for a house like this. I felt bad because the seller was older than I thought to be, but I couldn't blind side her. I did not go along the tour just to not buy the house when already I knew it was out of the circle, so I tried to be nice as I told her, "No thank you," and left.

Chapter Eleven

Monday rolls around. The houses that I saw yesterday were okay, but the second really stood out. I've decided to keep searching until I know exactly which house I prefer.

It's the afternoon. School ended an hour ago and I don't want to wait until it's too late to go house shopping, then Mom would get curious.

And.

I.

Can't.

Lie.

The kitchen smells weird. It's this insane mixture of milk and salt. I scrunched up my nose, "How much salt did you use for what?" I ask.

"This," Mom said, turning around with dough between her fingers. Something about that doesn't look or smell right. Instead of it balling up, the dough just slimes its way through and through Moms hands, and sometimes it splattered so hard I had to duck. How does dough even splatter?

"That is bizarre."

"Well, it's your supper."

I look to the floor instantly. Then Mom turns back to the counter and I add, "By the way, can I use the truck?"

"Embril, what for?"

No, don't ask that question.

"Rim took it somewhere," Rachel answers. She too has a dough of slime inside her fingernails Eew!

Instead of forcing the question, Mom collided with Rachel on the way to the sink and my Mom dropped the slime dough which burst found its way across the kitchen to my shoes.

"Shoot!" my Som shouts.

"Hey," I say almost scolding her.

Mom doesn't look at me.

"It's okay, I've done that many times-

Rachel starts to reassure my mother that the slime dough can be cleaned up, but I didn't listen. My eyes found themselves glancing toward the living room.

Cameron sits with his legs thrown out on the couch watching TV, with a bowl of ice cream in his hand.

I know that we aren't on the best of terms, but I have no transportation, and Cameron does.

"Hey Cam-eron."

He doesn't correct the way I said his name, or ever acknowledge that I'm there. Instead, Cameron ignored me and stared straight into the metal box that contains entertainment in front of him. I sigh.

Then I perked up, put a smile on my face, even blinked a few times before asking what comes next, "Will you go house shopping with me?"

That seemed to get his attention.

"What?! House shopping?! Do your parents know about this? Does Andrew?"

So he is best buds with Andrew now and I can't be, perfect.

"No, but---

"Why do you want to leave?"

It's silent.

I was not expecting Cameron to ask that question, I'm completely surprised, does he *not* want me to leave?

"No, I will not go house "shopping" with you," he puts quotations around the word shopping and then I realize that I have irritated him so much that we almost got into a fight, he almost yelled at me. I don't think I can handle seeing that side of Cameron.

I rejected the tear slipping from my eyes, I wiped at them and then tried to find another way to use my energy, to change the tone of this situation and then the light bulb revealed itself to me.

"Fine," I said standing up hoping that my eyes were not red, "I will just have to drive your truck then," I turned and headed for the door. I'm surprised that I made it outside. He didn't come after me.

My ears were now getting hot. How could that have not made him choose to go?

I slumped to the steps, not moving my feet. I guess this is the time that a fictional character would start to cry, but I am not a fictional character, I'm Embril Jack, and I am standing up to march back into that house and demand that he goes with me.

Instead, I realize that I would freeze when I got to him, with that puzzled look on his face. I'd rather see him smile.

Just then, the door slammed behind me and I quickly turned tolook. Cameron's face iwas red too. He lifted his right hand to his forehead and let a big breath escape.

"Thank goodness you haven't left yet. It took me a while to realize what you said."

A smile tugs at the corner of my mouth but I held it back. "So, are you coming then?" I said, and pushed my hands to my hips and stared at him. I never thought my voice would sound like that.

"I'm driving," he said and raced me to the door.

Chapter Twelve

It's lunch on Tuesday. Through first and second block, I ended up reading *The Fault In Our Stars*. I read though a bunch of it so I'm super close to the end. Normally, it takes me a week to start and finish a book but life has gotten difficult and I have wanted save as much reading pages as possible.

Cameron is sitting across from me. When we were in the truck yesterday, I finally got him to lighten up and we are back to normal. Well, we were back to normal until this happened.

"Just go say hi to her."

"Cameron, hi isn't going to work, look at her, she's too busy talking to notice me, plus I'm going to look like an idiot standing by a table trying to talk to someone when they are paying no attention," I took a breath then, that was a lot to say.

"No you won't, trust me and just go."

There was no way I would have gone, but Cameron said 'trust me' and I can't help the fact that I do, and it would be like lying if I didn't get up then, so I stood and walked slowly as ever to the table Cameron told me to go to.

I remember that I felt awkward standing there like I was, I was leaning over to say hi like Cameron instructed.

There was a twist.   I did not expect her to talk back, especially not as soon as she did. I guess I expected her to turn her head and whisper something to the guy sitting next to her, but I sure did have it wrong.

"Hello, what's your name?"

"Embril."

Someone on the other end of the table laughed, I looked up at him but ignored it all the same.

"What's yours?"

"Shasta Franks," she smiled.

"Okay, well see you 'round."

"Kay," Shasta turned just as quickly back to her friends as she turned to look at me.   Her dark skin matched the others that sit with her, and I wouldn't fit in, so I don't know why Cameron sent me to her. Now to think of it, I wonder if Cameron gave her a heads up, but I don't want to fight, so I will keep it to myself.

"Okay, now what?"

"See that girl?" Cameron lifts his finger straight behind me. She was also facing away, only three tables back.

"That close?" I asked. Feeling noxious, Cameron gets to witness this one.

He nods, so I tried to remember the training he gave me in the truck yesterday about what to do, and headed for the table.

That's when it threw me downhill.

"Hi," I had started.

The girl looked up at me with the ugliest face and said, "Excuse me? Who are you talking to? Who do you think I am? Who do you think *you* are?"

This startled me, I know that Cameron said something about this, to just walk away, but she insulted me, "I think I was just saying hello, is that so bad?"

"Yes, no one that I don't like talks to *me!*"

The people at her table started to nod in agreement. This girl has some serious problems, thinking too highly of yourself is highly dangerous. It could become suicidal once you realize what you've done and whom you have been. This is too scary and for me to just let it go on was even worse and is *wrong*. I had to do something about it. I had to try to help her.

"Sorry that you don't like me 'cause you've never talked to me a day in your life. Keep being stuck up like that and you will end up in a bad place." I remember that I tried to sound more nice than mean but now it seems like I was threatening her, which is bad, it's *real* bad.

"Oh no, you have done it! Joshua get me the Laser Beam!" her eyes got big.

"I'm not the one acting like a perfect manic! And how is a…a laser beam going to hurt me?"

"Josh!"

This is when people were starting to look.   This dude named Josh or Joshua, who knows, who care, brought out a gigantic Laser Beam.   He pointed it right at me but he stepped away and the girl I was having a word fight with took his place.

"This specific Laser Beam....

She starts into a science lesson talking about how much power can be zapped into a person, it sounded ridiculous to me, so I tuned her out and stood there until several SRO's were coming in our direction.   I stood up straight like I was scared to move, but then the girl pushed a red button on top and I was shot with the Laser.   Then I really couldn't move.

I shut my eyes as I hit the floor, then I thought of Cameron, did he know this would happen? Did he set me up for failure, for the SRO's to take me away and put me in a place? Like *this?*

I came back to reality.   That was the story I just told the guidance counselor, leaving the particular stuff about Cameron out of it.   Though now I still feel stiff, even though the immobilization has drifted away.   Yet it still feels real, and every word I told her is also real.

Why would Cameron set me up to talk to her? Did he know she would go off?   How can I forgive him?   He did forgive me, so I must try, I must start trying *now.*

Chapter Thirteen

THE COUNSELOR, Mrs. Mush… yes, I now it is a weird last name…told me that I now have detention for two days. Not because I was stiffened, unable to move for minutes and now feel terrible like if I move too suddenly, I will throw up everywhere, but because I apparently started it. She thinks that I did threaten her, though that was never my intention. She believed it that way.

So now I feel like I have detention, not because I should have walked away, but because she doesn't believe me.

That is how I learned to forgive Cameron, I forgave him without even asking if he set that up because I know he told me the right thing to do, and I chose not to.

That's what happened yesterday. Today is Wednesday and now I am in detention.

"Okay, this is detention!" Yells a teacher that I don't recognize. She stands in the front of the room and I already can tell she isn't happy to be here, "I am Mrs. Friezner and you *will* follow the rules I have written on the board for you." Mrs. Friezner tells us the rules without even turning her back to read them. She stands facing us the whole time, which is something I find rather creepy.

My thoughts leave me and I flick my eyes to the board to read the rules with her:

One: NO Talking!

Two: NO Gum!

Three: NO Getting Up!

Four: NO Food, Drinks, Etc…

Five: NO Escaping!

Mrs. Friezner pauses to add something to number five, "Which you will be punished for because I have eyes, *everywhere.*"

Then continues:

Six: NO Bathroom Breaks!

Seven: NO Texting!

Eight: NO Weapons!

Nine: NO Pranks!
AND
Ten: NO Sign Langue!

In my personal opinion, it sounds like a pretty crazy rule list. Never would I expect something like sign Language and bathroom breaks being a problem in detention, of all places. Though if she put them up there, it must have been done and ended badly before.

I began to wonder why she had written them down if she had them all memorized, then I looked around me and found my answer. There were people already breaking the rules, but that isn't who I am.

"Hey, what are you in here for?"

A girl with black lipstick and black painted fingernails leaned over to ask me this question. I clearly understand why she is here, I obviously don't belong in this room. My story is a little lopsided. Meaning that I am right, I should not be here, though someone else thinks I am wrong.

My story is not something I want to be laughed at, so I chose to be a different person for a second, I chose to be that dressed cute girl who doesn't look like trouble, but really is, "None of your business!"

I didn't shout, yell or scream. Because that would be in violation of the rules, though I am talking, so that's one rule broken.

I spat the words so hard at her trying to get her to believe that I'm in the right place, that spit flew out of my mouth and hit her in the eyebrow.

Oops, I wanted to cover my mouth and apologize, but that would be too right of me, so I pretended that didn't happen and looked forward.

"I see."

The girl mumbled and then left the seat she was sitting in.

"You are not to get up!" the teacher apparently gave herself the right to yell.

I expected Mrs. Friezner to do something else, but the girl stayed quiet so the teacher did too.

Fifteen minutes later, I am bored out of my mind. We've been sitting here in the silence and I'm afraid I will start to have an anxiety attack. The thing is to stay focused or distracted, so I lift my head from my desk with writing scribbled across it and found my sight to the book shelf.

I stared at it for a moment, my eyes traced the shelf up and down, up and down. There was something missing.

Finally, I took my eyes away. The books reminded me of my library, the one I use to have. The one that is so big, I still haven't read them all, is now burnt, gone.

In that moment I wanted to find Dustin and make him pay for ruining my life. Then I thought of Cameron. I couldn't hurt my friend that way, so revenge is out of the question.

My eyes started to wander again. This time, I found a big book on a different shelf behind the podium in front of the room.

Something tells me that was the book missing from the other shelf.

Then I thought of my letter to myself. The one I wrote in third grade, of my dreams to have read every book and rode a pony. This time that one dream sticks out to me, to write a book.

That letter got burnt up just like everything else. Yet, I still remember exactly what it said and the exact handwriting it was written in. This memory isn't as bad as the others. It should not exist, but it does and the book I will start writing today and eventually finish, will always remind me of that letter.

Mrs. Friezner never wrote a rule regarding to pencils and paper. I dug out my things and then I realized that I have to think first. So I twirled my pencil through my fingers until I decided what kind of story to write.

My home was something I loved, something I cared about and adored. This was not revealed to me until I lost it.

Tears did not come, I told myself this is a happy memory so that is what it became. I remembered bits and pieces of my life as pictures of the past flood back like a slideshow. Some things never came back to me though, say I would remember a time when my family came over for birthdays, dinners or a party for the football games, whole details were forgotten. Then I knew exactly what to write about… a children's book!

★★★

The story is a perfect lesson to learn. For kids to know this information is now my goal. It is something for me to try my best to get across. It feels so necessary. This story may be a tragedy to some people, even though it is not written that way, it is a lesson to kids, to appreciate their belongings, to not steal, to not be greedy and even to the people/kids that already feel alone and unappreciated. I want them to know that I felt connected to my house once it burnt down. I was not alone, I had my house, it loved me back, we shared memories. My house was my friend.

I'm back home. Well, not my home. The memory of my house no longer saddens me, for now I know that what my house and I had is a memory that should not be forgotten and never will it be. I have a book that will remind me of what I lost that is so important.

I came straight home after detention to continue my story. Since it is a children's book, it doesn't have to be very long, and by the looks of it now, I should finish it tomorrow, probably in detention itself. I will have something to do that way.

Andrew walked into my room so I put down my pencil and leaned back in the chair at my desk, stretching.

"Need something?" I asked. It hasn't been normal for Andrew to come into my room since we've been living here. I knew it was because he is mad at me, but why is he in here now?

"Nah, I just wanted to say that I'm sorry, and will you forgive me?"

Andrew didn't look at me the entire time he spoke, so I let the smile on my face grow as the conversation went on.

"For what?" I ask clasping my hands.

He rolls his eyes, "Embril?" he looks up at me then instantly back to the wooden floor as if that were a mistake, but he explained himself.   "For being mad at you. I was getting over being mad at you for being an idiot to run into a burning house, then you flip your kayak and almost…

"But then I was trying to see it from your perspective and I see that you didn't want the house to go and I know that you barely have experience in kayaking, so I am sorry."

Andrew has a few friends that let him borrow a kayak and asked him to go on trips where they kayak rivers and such.   I forgot about that, I forgot he was already experienced.   He was right for being mad at me for the house, but the kayaks?   I never will understand how he could have been so blind.

"So am I forgiven?"

Andrew was still staring at my floor, but I could see his eyes.   It looked like he was pleading with me.

"Yes."

"Awesome!" Andrew looks up and pumps his fist in the air, "Thanks Em, bye."

Without anything else, he ran out my door and I fell out of the chair.

"Why do I have to be so clumsy!" I yelled.

"Ha-ha!"

That was Andrew's voice, I guess he wasn't far down the hallway and heard me fall.

Night fell.   The writing process defiantly is different from reading a book. Which reminds me of *The Fault In Our Stars*.

I plan to read the end tomorrow during school.   As of right now, I yawn and head towards my bed.

★★★

"It's Thursday already?" I asked as Cameron placed his bowl in the sink.

"Yeah, wish it were Friday."

"Wish it were Saturday."

"Same," Andrew agrees with me.

"Well then," Cameron says and then my dad walked into the kitchen for a second cup of coffee. "Don't wish your life away kids," he says.

Then each of us three walk out in an 'orderly fashion.

I giggled once we got to the living room and Cameron just stared at me.

"What?" I asked but I couldn't keep myself from laughing.

"Nothing," he answers.

Next thing, Andrew and I are racing to the passenger seat in Cameron's truck. Of course, Cameron is driving so he walked like normal, until I climbed in the driver's seat because I lost to Andrew.

"Hey, hey, no get out of there!" Cameron yelled and joged toward me.

He stopped, "Get out," Cameron waved his thumb in the opposite direction of the vehicle.

I looked him dead in the eye and said, "Make me."

So he did, Cameron sat on top of me crushing my legs and pushing my head against the seat, so it's hard to breathe. Then my heart picked up speed and I pretended to suffocate.

"What's wrong?" Cameron freaks out and jumped off to see if Iwas okay. It worked.

"Nothing," I smile and headed for the back. We sang to the radio until we entered the schools parking lot.

Chapter Fourteen

The first of third block had been going for a while. I say first, because in the middle of the block, we have lunch and then come back to third.

The teacher put us into groups to assign each other parts for a project...parts as in our job in the assignment.

It's a difficult process. All around me were groups of four but I was one of the last people to get assigned so I was in a group of three.

I covered my ears. Other students are arguing with one another left and right, the teacher is not doing anything about it either. He is sitting at his desk with his feet propped up, reading a magazine. Who even reads magazines anymore? Certainly not in this century.

I got along with my partners well. Each of us wanted a different job. So that's what we got, though we seem a little too easy to work. I'm not sure if anyone was lying.

As the class went on, I opened my book and tried to read discreetly. The other people in my group looked at each other and then the girl puts her head down on the desk, as the next one follows.

That was weird.

Finally, I read the last word of *The Fault In Our Stars* and take a deep breath. I hope I don't need another distraction for a good while, or ever, but with my bad luck, *that won't happen.*

So I hope that it will be easy to find another distraction when another disaster comes around, then the bell for lunch rings.

★★★

Lunch was okay. Cameron rambled on about something involving new technology rumors to Andrew as I sat there and ate, feeling alone. They invited me to join in on the conversation, but I know nothing about electronics, so I pretended to listen.

It was getting close to the bell for third block to dismiss. My teacher decided he wasn't finished reading the tiniest magazine I have ever seen, not to mention he probably did the same in the last two blocks he's had.

Most people agreed to jobs they didn't want, then complained about it. Others still argued and the rest fell asleep. I was one of those people. I woke just in time for the bell. I fist-bumped the girl in my group that woke me, in favor, and darted to my last class.

In block four, we had a test. Nope, not fun. Though I got through it faster than I had expected, the test wasn't as fun as anyone would think it to be, and it didn't get any easier.

It took forever for the three o' clock bell to ring. I tried to walk as slow as possible to the detention room but several administrators were behind me, picking up the pace for everybody.

Detention was the same as yesterday, but not the same. The rules were still on the bored but written in different marker, Mrs. Friezner read off the rules again and caught everyone she saw that was not obeying. She really has more eyes that you could possibly think of.

Instead of letting my own eyes wander, I went straight to writing, which I got most of it done.

Now I'm home in my room and I just edited the last bit of the children's book I've worked so hard to finish.

For a second I was shocked, I didn't know what to do. As I sat and stared at the words in front of me, I finally realized that my work was done.

"Guys!" I start to scream and finally jump from the chair, "Guys! Hello? Hey! Anyone? Please give me some attention!"

My screams of joy turned into anger, no one would answer back to me. So, I raced myself down the steps and that's when they saw me.

"Guys! Guess what? I finished the book!"

"Oh, that's awesome," said Mom.

Hardly anyone seemed excited or proud of me, that was a huge let-down, but at least I am proud of myself.

Then I let my face harden.

"We will have to send it to get it published then," Mathew smiled at me. I guess he saw my lips purse and felt bad for me. Though that made me even more mad.

"We should go celebrate, then. Let's go bowling." Cameron was the only person who seemed to be giddy, as he bounced on the balls of his feet. I am not sure if it is because of me, or the celebration idea.

★★★

So we went. It was dark by the time we got there, but the bowling alley was dark too and was lit up with neon lights.

"How do I do this again?"

I had to turn around and ask for instructions for the fifth time. I've never been bowling before, but it seems fun by the looks of the others in the room.

My family sighed while Rachel laughed. Mathew and Cameron just sat there fiddling with the screen so I bet they weren't paying attention.

Andrew's sigh turned into a weird laugh just before he said, "I got it."

Andrew showed me how to hold the ball and which arrow to put it on as I push it down the lane.

After my first roll, I was sure that I wasn't going to be winning the game, but I tried to not let it get to me.

It was Mathew's turn next. He stood and elegantly made his way up to his bowling spot. I've never seen anymore more fancy walking in my entire life. Where was he born?

Mathew hit a strike, "Can you beat that Rim?"

My Dad released himself from the spin chair and received his own ball. Then he let go of it and watched as it knocked down all but two pins, one on the right, other on the left. That means he has to choose one with the next throw. I could never do that. The pins are equal. How could I simply chose one over the other? Then I listened to my own thoughts and decided that I was thinking in a weird way.

"Yes!" Cameron pumped his fist down from the air as he let everyone know that he was in first place, "Won't be up there for too long sweetheart."

It was Rachel's turn next, she also was elegant on her walk toward the lane, but she didn't have as much style as Mathew did.   I guess there really isn't any point to observe this.   I would not win this game with a certain way to walk, even if the Halls family thought it did.

Thirty minutes passed.   Andrew came in second but Mathew came in first place for the first game.   I watched each player and observed their technique, the way they held the ball, the way they walked, and the way some of them crossed their legs and turned around in a full circle after their roll.

I watched everyone in the room, not just my family and my Dad's friends' family.   I guess that explains why I am suffocating in a group hug right now. I won.

The second game winner in bowling was something I never would have dreamed about being. This position is really a high point for me, a new memory that I will never let go of.

Chapter Fifteen

I awoke from a nightmare.   The house that belongs to the Hall family, was now being burnt, just like mine, but it was different.   This time I didn't care about any lost belongings, so that is what happened.   In the dream, whatever I wanted to happen did, but it was always the wrong choice.

I'm glad I had the nightmare though, it reminded me of the day I went house shopping and how much I want to get out of here.   I went to my desk to pull out the drawer and dig out the paper with the house I circled.

"Mom, I have something for you."

"Really?" she whiped her head around and I waved Dad over to see what it is that I've come up with.

I showed them the page and watched as both of their eyes grew, wide.

"What? It's perfect! It has just enough bedrooms and a pretty kitchen.   Look! Back here is even an extra space where we could build a new library and stalk it!" I was getting too excited.

Andrew overheard and walked into the hallway with us, "Rooms? What?"

"Kids, I'm afraid that it will be longer than expected.   The insurance doesn't pay it all, we just don't have the money yet."

Mom looked down when Dad finished talking.   It looked like maybe she was ashamed.

"Oh," was all I could manage to choke out, but Andrew, just stood there, astonished.

"We could raise the money! I can start-

"Embril, this is our job let us handle it," my Mom cut off my sentence before I could finish, then both my parents walked away from me.   I called them back, because I have to.   I refuse to not get to help with this. "It was *my* house too," I muttered, just before Andrew unglued himself from the door frame.   I called a family meeting in the living room.   These people aren't separated to me anymore, they are *all* my family.

"I have decided to come up with a way to raise money for my new house." I had to make the quick decision to not pause, because Mom looked worried. "We will have a bake sale."

"Well that's nice," Rachel immediately replied, I guessed that was her way of telling me to get out of her home.

"Plus the money from your book," says Mathew as he walks in from the door, maybe he heard me all the way outside.

I looked at him rapidly, "*What?*"

"Not right now," my Mom gots up and yanked me into the kitchen by my elbow, "Ow!"

She ignored me. "How dare you? A child of mine will *not* embarrass me like that. You just invited yourself to use other people's ingredients and their kitchen and their supplies. That is not the kind of people we are."

I swallowed hard and looked at Dad, who was walking into the kitchen as well. "Keep it down, and I like this idea, Georgia. We do need some help.

I wanted to say that I was confused, but I wasn't. I just never had given thought to what I was asking Rachel to do for me... the person she despises for no apparent reason, and for the person who is living with her.

"Rachel didn't seem to have a problem with it," I said in the lowest voice possible, not in a talk back manner, but in a convincing way.

"Fine, I will be right back."

Mom came back into the kitchen with Rachel and they started to get supplies and ingredients for cookies, cupcakes, brownies, pies, anything sweet that could get someone's attention.

"Embril? You in here?" Cameron walked in holding a sheet of paper in the air.

"Um, Yeah?"

"Look at this."

He handed me the paper and at the top in bold printing it said:

Story Accepted

"No way!" I shriek.

"What happened?" Mom asked.   I told them just as it slipped from my tongue.   We gathered into another group hug and I just remembered, I should get income from this, it can be put toward our house!

★★★

We brought a table and a few chairs out to the front yard, along with all of the sweets we had baked. Several people flew by in their cars without hesitation, but almost the same number of people stopped to take a look.

By Five o' nine in the afternoon we had received a donation of two thousand dollars!

"Embril that's it! we have what we need!"

My Mom told me about the donation and I beckoned Andrew and Cameron to come out and share the leftover cookies with me.   Then it started to rain.

"Aw no!" someone yelled.   I'm not sure who, but I disagreed.

"Rain is rain and rain can be fun."   I happened to spot a mud hole in the yard to my right, so I grabbed Andrew and we fought, slinging mud everywhere.

Later, I got into the shower to clean up.   Then I slid into bed and just laid there in the dark to clear my mind, until Cameron stepped in.

Chapter Sixteen

Today I am wearing my shoes that cover the tops of my toes.   Any other day, when I wasn't walking around the neighbor hood after the rain, I would have worn them.

"Cameron, do you know what that is?" I bent over to look at the sidewalk closer.   Cameron followed, squinting.

"Um, no I don't think so."

"It's called a centipede," I said, trying not to judge him...he *does* live in the suburbs.

Last night, Cameron decided to ask me to take a walk with him in the neighborhood today.   I don't expect it to take long, but I put my hair into a pony tail anyway.

"See that house right there?"

Cameron lifted his index finger to a house that's on my right.   It's small, but all houses through here are that way, so I put that thought behind me.

"Yeah...and?"

"Don't be mean, this is part of the friend-spree." He put his finger down as he spoke.

"Sorry, I didn't know we were still doing that.

"Yes, oh and how are things with you and Dustin?"
Wish he did had not brought that up.

"I haven't seen him around."

"Oh," Cameron says and tilted his head to the ground.   What if they weren't so close? Would what I'm doing make him sad, even less than he would be if he found out now?   Or would he have skipped Dustin completely with the friend-spree?

Cameron continued, "That is Cathy Barrel's house, but her daughter is someone you're going to talk to.   Her name is Sydney Barrel."

"Okay."

We walk for a few more sinutes before we reached the next house.   Cameron told me the names of the people that I'm supposedly going to talk to.   Apparently these people will become my new friends, and I'm glad that I have never heard of any of them before.

As we walked back to Cameron's house, he gave me a quiz. "That is Miles Radish's house and the next to the left belongs to James Mathis."

I clapped my hands together as Cameron congratulated me.

"So who are your friends?"

"Sydney Barrel, James Mathis, Miles Radish and Shasta Franks," I lifted head from the ground to look at him, then he threw his hands in the air and looked up at the sky.

I just looked at him, waiting for some sort of answer as to what I did.

"What about me?"

"Oh, yes and definitely you!"

Cameron looked back at the ground and keept walking. I followed.

I waiedt a few blocks before speaking, "What's wrong?"

"Nothing."

"Cameron don't lie to me, you've been upset for seven blocks now."

We walked a long way...

"I don't know really, just, once you start gaining friends, I lose mine."

Oh.

It's me, it's definitely me. His friends are leaving him because he is hanging out with the homeless girl, the only homeless girl in our school. But why did he choose *me* over *them?*

I didn't say anything else. Instead, I held his hand as we walked the last half mile home. Something about that made my heart start racing.

Chapter Seventeen

It's Tuesday. We've been waiting for the money for my children's book to come in the mail. I've received some but not much, and the last letter told me they were sending more.

As I wait for my book to become famous, *which will never happen,* (sigh) I go to school and try to be brave. This meeting people, is not something I am very good at, and according to Cameron, we start today.

In my opinion, I think we started a long time ago, and we argue about this, 'No, no it's just beginning!' 'You are insane.'

It's Tuesday. Which means that yesterday afternoon was the time that Cameron took me on a walk and gave me pop quizzes on random people's home's.

"Okay, go talk to her," Cameron pushes me toward Sydney. First block hasn't started yet. Apparently Cameron thinks this is a good time to make friends, though I think it is a little weird. I'm randomly walking up to people and starting conversations, does that seem suspicious in some sort of way?

"Hey," I smiled at Sydney and she says hey back. Then I go blank, what should I say? Nothing crosses my mind so I think back to the "lessons" about friends that Cameron told me, complement her.

"I like your shoes," but do I really?

"Thanks, I'm Sydney."

Right, I could have introduced myself.

"Embril."

I stand there not knowing what to say next. Sydney turns away from me and starts into the conversation with her other friends. For a while I was still there, trying to fit in, but the conversations they talked about jumped all over the place, I simply never knew what to say. Even if I did, I bet no one would listen.

"Well that happened," I said as I reached Cameron.

"What did?"

"Felt out of place," I said crossing my arms.

"You can't possibly feel out of place everywhere, with all the options I'm giving you," he says mimicking my position.

We stare each other down until the seven fifty- five bell rings, five minutes until class starts.

Without us saying any other words, we turn in different directions and I throw myself down the stair rail.

"Hey! No sliding!" a teacher yelled at me, but I ignored her and kept going until I stopped at my class. I can't believe I just slid down the rail. Others do it all the time, but me? I'd never. I must be changing into a new person.

The eight o' clock bell rang so I stepped as quickly as I could inside the door and everyone stared at me as I sprinted to my seat.

Stop looking at me!

I shouted to everyone inside my head, but of course they can not hear me.

Mr. Tidewalk came in next and suddenly everyone's eyes switched to him, *thank you.*

I was the last to give my attention. It is quiet as ever, which made me realize that it's going to be a slow day. Might as well strap in my seat belt and hang on for the ride.

★★★

As I believed it would, first block went slowly. So did second block.

I saw Sydney in the hall way towards the cafeteria and we smiled at each other. I guess I should go talk to her, but what would I say?

"Hey."

It's Shasta, she came up behind me so I jumped and without thinking twice of the words, I blurt out, "Hey! Careful you scared me!"

That's when I have a miniature heart attack inside. Do people not say things like that? Or do people these days just don't get scared, especially not that easy. What will Shasta think of me now, that I'm some psycho?

"Well it was my intention," she smiles.

Maybe my reaction wasn't as wrong as I thought it was.

We walk into the cafeteria together and I sit down by Cameron while she goes to the line.

"So, how's it going?"

"Perfect," I answered to Cameron as I rolled my eyes.

"Don't give me sass," he strikes back.

"Sorry king of the attitude," I remark.

Cameron smiled and then pointed to a table all the way across the space in the middle of the cafeteria. This space often separates the sporty kids and the smart kids. Not to say that sporty kids aren't smart, though smart kids tend to be more smart and their future does not depend on a game.

"That's Miles Radish, baseball player."

I take a deep breath, I practically know where he lives now, "Okay."

As I begin my walk, I almost trip over a milk carton. My face got red hot and I wanted to run, but Cameron's attempt to catch me made something about it seem less embarrassing, so I go on.

"Hello," I said once I reached my destination. Hello? People don't say that, what am I doing?

"Um, hey," he seems surprised, and weirded out, I frown.

"I'm Embril."

"Miles," he says and tilts his head back like he's nodding at me. Then he looks at his friend and I think they're making fun of me.

Instead, I shake it off and something about the way he's acting makes me tell myself to *loosen up*.

That's what I did, and the words just slipped right out of my mouth, "I've been challenged by a friend, um, so I have to talk to random people." As I talk, my pony tail bobs up and down.

Miles and his friends seemed to like the truth, but Miles talked for them, "Ah, then come sit with us."

"I can for a bit," I said and took the closest seat. My legs were about to go numb from standing.

For the first five minutes I'm just sitting there staring at the ground. Miles and his friends are talking about the weirdest things. I just have nothing to say. Then I realize this is quite how I am with my old group of friends. I honestly don't know if it's just because I am a quiet person or because I'm honestly not confident in myself?

So I lifted my head to start a new conversation, but then I heard a loud "Oh!" sound. It came from the far right hand corner of the room so I whipped my head around to see what was happening, but everything was normal.

A second more and now the table where I'm sitting, all guys, does the same thing. I really don't want people to see me with my mouth in the shape of an "O," so instead I laugh at Miles ridiculous face.

"You have a pretty smile," Miles's friend says looking straight at me.

"Yeah, I wonder if what you said was true, you could have just wanted to talk to us," said another. I looked around the table to see everyone in complete agreement, besides Miles himself, so I focus on him.

"Guys chill," he says but no one listens.

"Yeah, sorry, that's not it and I have to go bye."

I practically run back to my own table with Cameron who seems to have another friend waiting on me. Were those guys back there flirting with me? How do I respond to that?

When I finally got to my table I forget all about the full milk carton that was on the floor. I was walking so fast that it was blurry as I tripped over it again. Though this time it was worse, I actually fell.

★★★

"Ow!" I said, as the nurse adjusted my foot.

Cameron helped me to the nurse office and his friend, who I found out is James Mathis, (Math club leader, *ironic*), came too.

"It's just a bruise, no serious damage," the nurse reminded me.

I understand that, it's just a silly milk carton but that makes no sense of why it would hurt me.

Was I being attacked again? Dustin? What is he up to?

"Okay you are good to go," the nurse takes my ice pack off and sends me on my way.

James and Cameron slung their back packs over their shoulder and Cameron waits for me to stand up while James gets my back pack.

"It's two minutes until the two-thirty bell," James said, checking his watch.

It really doesn't feel like I've been in the nurse' office for that long, but I went to the last lunch, so I guess that is why it is already time to go.

"Thanks guys, really you don't have to help me."

"We want to," Cameron quickly says before James could respond.

I'm quiet. There isn't anything I have to say to that, if they want to let them.

We are the first people in the hall and we make it close to half-way before other students start to flood the place.

I'm glad that gave us a head start, but now I feel like I am suffocating in a building full of people who need my failures in order to live.

Then I wonder if my old group of friends would be here helping me with this right now. All this time, for about four years, I have been telling myself that I do not need friends, I can do it on my own and that friends are too much trouble, too much drama. Yet I have friends today, and even though I may not need them, they aren't bad to have in the first place. Without my friends, I would have no memories of the things that happened at school, I would have no jokes to tell.

Friends are people that are kind and they help you become who you are today, friends help you with your confidence, personality, your smarts and believe it or not, your physical strengths and weaknesses.

Without my friends, I would not be Embril Magenta Jack.

Chapter Eighteen

"Embril! Come Quick!"

I heard Andrew yelling at me from upstairs. The problem is I have no guess at what for, so I toss my phone on the bed and skip steps on my way down.

"What? What is it?"

"We got the house!"

"Hu-huh?"

I'm stunned. I just stood there with my mouth peeling down to the carpet.

"We got the house, you know the one that you circled, we had enough money, oh, and here." Andrew handed me an envelope that read in bold letters:

To Build A House:
Fifty-Four dollars.

My book! My book money, "Fifty-four doll-

I can barely finish my sentence, "Dollars?"

"Yep, we are moving in tomorrow at three, so go pack."

I have to admit, out of all the work it took for my parents to get us all back on our feet, and by how long we have been here, Andrew seems the most excited to get a new home.

Out of all the for sale houses out there...they bought the one that I wanted the house that I chose.

My feet left the ground as I jumped up and raced Cameron up the steps.

"Help me pack?"

"That's the plan."

When we get to my room I stopped mid-floor.

"Um, woops," I slowly turn my head back to look at Cameron and give him my shameful facial expression. The room was a mess.

"It doesn't matter," he said and walked over to my closet.

I tried not to let it bother me as we stripped the clothes from the small space, but it wouldn't leave my mind.

"Okay now for the shoes," he said and dropped to the floor.

"Alright," I agree but let out a sigh. This is making me sweat.

"Hmm, it's still here," Cameron says and I find him on the floor staring at the wall.

"I know, the colors are not really my style," I said trying to be nice about the way these walls are painted, but he doesn't say anything until I scoot closer to him.

"No, I meant this," he pointed to the little drawing of a house, with the boy and a dog.

Cameron smirked, "I drew this," he smoothed over the drawing with his right hand. "I wanted a sibling when I was younger but my parents refused, so I asked for a dog, though I never received one."

"When I met you, it was the biggest shock. I had always wanted a sister."

"Me too," is all I could say.

★★★

On Wednesday, Andrew and I skipped school. Our parents thought it was a good idea to stay and clean before we left for good. I'm sure we will visit, but we have a new home!

When Cameron got back from school he helped my family put our things in dad's truck and some in Andrew's.

"Thanks for helping," I told him.

"Thanks for being my friend."

"I thought you had friends, weren't the people you introduced me to your friends?"

"Ex friends," he pushed his eyes to the ground.

I was about to ask what happened but instead, Cameron talked before I did, "I don't want to talk about it."

"Well, why don't I call them and they can help us move in . Come on! I'm right here they can't hurt you," I tried to make everything seem okay.

"Do what you want but I can't promise I will be there when you need me."

I frown, "What's that mean? Cameron you are still helping us right?"

"Yeah, go ahead, call them," he crosses his arms and stares at the dirt again, so I picked up my phone and started dialing numbers.

"Great, see you there!"

I just got off the phone with Miles, he was the last person I asked, and thankfully, Shasta, Miles and James are coming.

Cameron rode beside me in my Dad's truck after we told Rachel and Mathew thanks for letting us stay. It was quieter than I expected but when we got there, my friends hugged me and we all brought things inside.

"Wow, this is a beautiful house," Shasta said.

"Well thank you Ms. It is my very own," I smiled at her being cocky, until James came up behind us with a tote box. "Really, are you paying for it?" he asked.

"Hey!" I shout back, and Miles came after James with another tote box. "Are you going to help at all?"

"Yes," I laughed and grabbed Shasta's arm to lead her to the truck.

My friends seemed a little weirded out that Cameron is here. I could see the tension but it isn't as thick as he made it seem.

When we had gotten everything inside the house, I noticed that Cameron was trying to distance himself from, well, everybody. He seemed mad at the world.

"Hey, cheer up," I said.

"Nah."

"Cameron please," I gave him my sad face, "these are your friends. Whatever happened, I'm sure that it is not unforgivable." I looked him in the eyes but he kept looking at the ground.

"Embril, they are your friends now, I am alone and that's okay."

"No, we are not doing this, you are doing exactly what I did in eighth grade. You are trying to convince yourself that you do not need friends. Do you see what you are saying? Cameron, you almost yelled at me for thinking the same way you are!

"You do not need friends, but they are everything you think that you don't have right now. You can make memories with them. I proved that to myself. Remember what it was like to laugh? That was fun right? Our friends make us laugh. We need to have a social life while we can, because it wont always be there."

I started taking deep breaths to calm myself. Cameron is the exact person who made me see how much friends can give you, and I just want him to have that. I want my best friend to see me as his friend. It's like he is refusing to look right in front of him, at me, I love him.

I actually love him because I don't want him to fall into the same place I was, he helped me get free, I have to help him, I *have* to.

Instead of saying anything else I put my hand into his and that's when he looked at me. I'm afraid he will push me away, but he doesn't.

"You are my best friend," I said, and every syllable that came out felt foreign to me, like it wasn't even real.

"Mine as well," he smiles at me

Our friends are staring at us now and slowly each of them walked to us as we formed a circle and cluttered into a group hug.

This is what friends are for. Friends are kind people who can tell you that you are forgiven without saying the words. Friends are people who you feel you can tell anything to and that is what life is about. Life is sharing everything with the people you love.

Chapter Nineteen

It was the first night of sleeping in a bed that is actually mine for a while, of sleeping in a bed that I don't have to make up every morning, a bed that I can throw myself on top of every day and wash the sheets with the scent of ocean.

We haven't gotten everything unpacked yet, but Mom is still making Andrew and me go to school.

After I ate breakfast and changed my clothes, I walked out to Andrew's truck where he was waiting for me.

"When are we getting your truck?" he sounded angry.

"Don't know," I answered and hopped in.

As we drove to school, the most coincidental thing happened.

We passed a house that was up in flames. I felt bad for the family who owned it; maybe they have nowhere to go. My eyes filled up with tears as I thought of the events of my own house burning... my memories. It's memories, and that brings me to what mMom said when she saw me, "What were you doing before this happened?

I feel determined now, determined to figure out, to really figure out how that happened.

My first source, Dustin.

★★★

School was terrible. I had a rough day. I was tripping over things and taking a lot of tests, which soon gave me a headache.

It did not take me long to want to get through today before I started my mystery quest.

The house that I now call my home feels wrong. When I walked in I half-way expected to see Rachel staring me down. Really, I don't know why she didn't like me, I had done nothing to her.

I hung my back pack on the hook and took a trip to the basement. It is the hottest part in the house. I know that Rachel's house has a basement that is freezing, but that must be because she never turns her air conditioning off. We hardly ever turn it on because my Dad thinks it's a waste of money, so for the past two days that I have been here, my fan has been on full blast. The basement looks dull. The floor and the walls are gray. Maybe some day I can paint the walls.

I examine the tiny closet in the far right corner of the room. It is quite big,...big enough to fit two people and storage.

I started to wonder why I wanted to come down here, so I turned around and walked back up the steps.

"Hey Embril, the Hall family wants us to go hiking with them tomorrow," my Mom told me when I reach the kitchen.

"Okay?"

"We all are going and so is Adoria."

"Alright that's nice," I said and just keep walking until I got to my room.

I laid down on my bed and thought of my old library. When can we install one here?

Then I think of the back room where the library could be and from there I think about the house. I took my own mental tour, imagining what it would look like once we have all of our decorations and furniture put it.

The back room will be turned into the library, then you could walk down a narrow hall way and to the right is another hallway, the one that leads you to Andrew's room and mine is on the other side.

If you go back into the first narrow hallway and keep walking until there is a doorway on your left, and in there is the living room. Walking across the living room you would find my Mom and Dad's room, which they have their own bathroom. Andrew and I have to use the one in the living room, close to the entryway. If you pass the front door, the house will take you to the kitchen, where there is another hallway that takes you to the door that goes into the basement, though if you skip the kitchen we have a side door that takes you to the porch and the back door is to the left of the back room.

I soon fell asleep without sliding into the covers. Our new house has no memories with us yet, and I refuse for it to have none.

★★★

The strap of my drawstring bag slid off my shoulder as I climbed up the rock. Cameron was behind me with Andrew and Adoria following him. I felt safe to know that he would not let me fall and get hurt. For most of the hike he has been behind me, with Rachel and Mathew in front. It was hard to see where I was going, but my parents were in front, leading the way.

In my opinion, the hike was good. No one got hurt and the trees were clearly marked so we could not get lost. Though I have the sense that the way things went with change, something could happen. I could smell rain and it kept getting darker by the second.

"Em, wait up," Adoria finally caught up to me after we passed the big rock a few ways back.

I heard Andrew mumbling something to Cameron but Adoria's voice drowned him out, "So I haven't seen you in a while."

"Right! I have missed you," I answered.

"Sorry about your house. It must not have been easy."

I lowered my head. Really, I am okay, but the sight of watching my house burn with no firefighters around to stop it, burned the memory back into my brain, and that thought isn't easy to push away.

"Thanks," I said without letting her know.

"It's raining," Andrew said and I looked up to the sky as it turned black, getting a drop of water in my eye during the process.

"I rubbed my right eye to keep my vision from going blurry, then the rain picked up.

"Everyone okay?" I hear my Dad shout, and then came multiple echoes of people reassuring their safety.

We stopped at a big tree, which does not do a very good job at keeping us dry.

"We are going to get wet either way," Cameron announcds but his Mom shushed him.

The rain slowed down so we started walking again.

We walked for a mile, climbing over rocks and hopping over lizards until the rain picked up again.

This time the rain doesn't slow down for at least twenty minutes, then it started to thunder, with little flashes of lightening.

"Hey," Cameron said, and I knew he iwa talking to me because he jogged to catch up and walk beside me.

So I looked up at him waiting for him to tell me something else, or just to start talking about anything else other than the storm happening all around us. We were in a dangerous spot.

"It's okay," Cameron said and that made me believe him.

It felt like an hour before the storm stopped. I honestly don't know how long it really was.

We got back into the line we had before and kept walking. I wondered how much more we had to go before turning around again, but it seemed we had a bigger problem.

"Can we climb over it?" I heard Mom trying to figure out a solution.

"No, it is too high," my Dad responded.

I pushed through to the front where my parents were, to see why we stopped.

My guess was that lightning was not on our side today. A tree had fallen over the trail...a big tree.

My Dad is right, I could see how we should not try to climb over it, but I could see my Mom's point too. The tree is way too close to the ground.

"What do we do?" Rachel asked.

"I guess we turn back," replied my Dad.

Then my heart sunk. I was really having a fun time, but then someone, something just had to go and attack me again. Why do all the bad things happen to me?

I don't understand, but this needs to stop. I'm not sure I can endure it much longer.

So my brain searched for a reason why I've been having to deal with all the bad situations, and I felt like I'm doing it alone, well, more like it was all meant for me somehow.

Next, it came to me and I had to say his name, even though it is crushing me to do this, "*Dustin*, watch your back".

Chapter Twenty

On Monday, I decided to wear my favorite shirt, the chevron patterned one. Perhaps it will make Dustin remember this day. The day I get revenge for his attacks on me, the day I will make sure he does not plan anything else forward.

I haven't really given much thought to how I would do this, but the day has come. I must figure out something. If Dustin runs fast, or at all like how he looks to be, there is no way possible this will ever work. My legs weren't invented for the running.

It wasn't until lunch time until I had come up with a plan. Dustin goes to my school, so it shouldn't be that hard. I think it would be best to leave school early so Cameron will not really have another choice but to let me leave.

"Hey Cameron," I started, "I'm going to walk home I don't feel very well."

"Why don't you take the truck? I will give you the keys."

"Thanks, but I haven't gotten my daily exercise," I can see how that was a little far-fethched. I walk every day from class to class.

"Alright."

Really I thought Cameron would say something else but he seemed to believe the story full-fledged.

I know where Dustin sits in the cafeteria, but in case Cameron saw me, I waited until Dustin threw his trash away so that I could ask his friends what his next class is.

That plan failed. Dustin got back to the table quicker than I have ever seen anyone do.

"Dustin will you come with me? I need to speak with you."

Dustin sat there, literally sat there staring at me. When it was obvious that I was starting to get agitated he spoke up, "I didn't do what you assume or anything else, I swear." He put his hands up as if to defend himself and I wasn't even two feet away from him.

"Explain Wal-Mart then?"

"Oh, umm....I just wanted to show you something we could have used for homecoming. I remembered seeing you in the club."

My entire weight felt like it was being sucked out of me. I felt my shoulders droop and my legs bend just before I fell to the floor. My head was hurting in a total pain of fire. I tried my best not to scream. I told myself I was still in school, and it would be even more embarrassing than when Cameron picked me up from the floor...like what he is doing now.

"What? Cameron...I..."

"Shush, we're going home."

★★★

The light in the room was too bright. It hurt when I squeezed my eyes open. The antiseptic smell of the hospital saturated the air. The smell is what scared me so much that I jumped. My Mom, who was only in the room besides the doctor, didn't notice I had waked up.

I blinked several times, but the blurriness would not disappear, so I gratefully shut my eyes again.

"Ma'am, I am sorry, but the facts here seem to tell us that your daughter has a concussion and you said that she has had two more in the previous year. If you are not careful, it could lead to head trauma." I squeezed my eyes as tight as I could Was it me? Were they really talking about me?!

When I opened my eyes again, the light hurt but the blurriness was gone. I saw Mom turn her head and walk over to me. "Oh dear," she said and started to stroke my hair.

"What's going on?" I asked, without sitting up.

"Cameron told us what happened at school," she expects me to believe that I know what happened before I woke up to a room of white lights? I let her think that. If

I didn't, she would either feel sympathy, be worried, or be heartbroken. I can't afford that.

I do remember trying to talk to Dustin, that he said something about being in the club together…and…it was….oh, Wal-Mart.

I believe that Dustin wouldn't try to hurt a stranger in such a public place. Really, I think he was telling the truth, I remembered having his full eye contact. They are a green/gray color.

However, I do not believe it wasn't him that tried to burn my house down. I will figure this out.

"Mom, did we ever call the firefighters to look at our house?"

"No, what brought this on sweetheart?"

"I'm just trying to think," I told her as we walked down the hall. She has to know I've found out the reason we were here by now.

This is my new plan…

Once I get in my room at my own house, alone, I will pick up my phone and probably hesitate for only a minute before dialing 911.

"Hello, you've dialed 911, what is your emergency?"

"I would like to speak with some firefighters. A while back, my house was burnt to the ground and I would like to figure out the reason."

"I will give them your number," the lady will respond, with the type of voice you would hear on a television.

"Thank yo-

Before I would be able to get the words out, the lady most likely would have hung up. I could get into heaps of trouble, but tomorrow I'm going home.

***

I walked to Andrew's room when I woke up. He was already up and eating a banana on his bed.

"Hey, I need to go get my truck….drive me?"

"I never thought you would want to go back there Em," he said.

"I just… I need my truck."

"Fine, give me two minutes."

I rushed back to my room and slipped on shoes.

The living room was empty but I still sneaked around.   It wasn't until my Mom hollered that I felt panic. I felt I was doing something wrong.

"Embril! Are you ready to go?"

I'm pretty sure that she was trying to take me back to the hospital. I am okay, seriously it's not like I can't speak. It took all I had in me not to answer.

"Andrew have you seen your sister? The doctor needs to see her," I could see Andrew's face from where I was.   He frowned and instantly looked to the floor.   "I haven't seen her."

Andrew then made his way past my Mom, who was standing frozen by the steps.

Then I crawled as close to the floor as I could get. Andrew opened the door and I walked out before he did.

When Andrew started up his truck, I was still buckling my seat belt. We pulled out of the driveway in no time!

"I'm going to take Adoria to the park to meet her family.   Come there when you're ready." Andrew was just telling me where he was so that we could face our Mother together.   I'm afraid that she really has no idea that I'm fine.   No pain bothers me besides unexpected head-pounding migraines.

"Okay," I told Andrew and the ride ended up being silent with the faint sound of the radio.

My mom texted me after we had been gone for only three minutes.

WHERE ARE YOU? DOCTORS APPOINTMENT!

Andrew took me to get my truck, be back soon. Feeling fine xoxo.

After I responded I turned the messaging to mute. I couldn't do this alongside the firefighters if my Mom was chewing me out for living my completely normal life.

When we turned onto the road closest to home, my heart started to fall.   It felt like I was pointless, there was no reason for coming here. I wanted to tell Andrew to turn around and just take me to the park, but I didn't. I had to figure out why Dustin had burnt my only home. What was it to him? Who was I to him? Who were my family or all the ancient china collections to him or even if it was Dustin who had my house burn to the ground...it could be....well, Michel. Perhaps he was just acting weird. He was only reading books in class to be more like me or give me a shouting hint. "Hey it was me. Put the pieces together. Don't you want revenge? I burnt your house to ashes!" I could see him saying those words. Though Michel Shrew doesn't have a reason either.

As Andrew pulled into our half-mile long drive way, I wondered if the firemen were already there, would they start investigating without my approval? Surely they wouldn't.

Andrew parked on the concrete and unlocked the door. Fair enough. The firemen were already there, but they hadn't even gotten out of their vehicles.

"Good luck. Sis."

"Yeah," I answered and half jogged to the fire trucks before Andrew drove away.

When I approached the long red vehicles, men in suits jumped out and waited silently for me to speak.

"Hello, I'm Embril Jack. Feel free to investigate whatever the need. I must know the cause of this problem if you have clues I'd like to hear them ASAP. You can go."

The people dispersed and I stood there the entire time, watching them search outside and inside. I heard them scattering about and using their equipment.

Then I dozed off. It felt like three hours before a person had spoken and when they did it was useful. "Found the source!" A man shouted as he threw off a face mask that no one else had worn.

"What is it!" I yelled, as I started toward the voice.

"Over here miss!" The man was inside...he was inside the kitchen. You mean something that happened in the kitchen was the cause of this mess? In that case it couldn't have been an outsider. That means no one else could have attacked me.   It means that it had to have been someone inside the house and not a non-family member was there that day.   It means that all those threats I said to Dustin, everything I did, the way I acted to him, the way I put Cameron in the friend spree situation was not even from a real cause....

"Ma'am?"

"Oh, yes?"

The man holds up a Ziploc bag filled with small pieces of black burnt ashes.

"Um, what? What is this?"

"It's the ashes of a popcorn bag. This seems to be the reason that your house had caught fire."

No....wait...this....no! Popcorn?! Who in the world would have fixed popcorn?   My brain started asking random questions that I just had to answer:

1. Who in the family likes popcorn?
    Me.
2. What time of day was it?
    Three-thirty.
3. Who eats at three-thirty?
    Me.

It was...it was me. It had to be me!! I burnt down my house? I burnt my home! I must have been so interested in the book I was reading that I forgot about my snack.   Then after I hit my head on my bed, I had forgotten.

I turned into a disaster right there.   Hot tears stained my face red.   Salt got in my mouth as I screamed.   I screamed and I yelled why did I have to jump to conclusions? Why did I assume it was Dustin? How could I blame it on him? The facts didn't even add up.   It made no sense.   I was angry and furious with myself.

The firemen walked back to their trucks and I was shouting so loud I didn't hear the engines start.

I started to pick up chunks of brick and throw them straight up into the air above me.   I slammed the bricks against the ground until they were buried.   I lined them up... brick by brick and punched them until my knuckles bled.

It was me! I destroyed it all! I took down my own memories, my own library, my own family's possessions. We lost everything we had ever owned and it was my fault... all because I wanted stupid popcorn at three-thirty!

I stayed there. I didn't bother about my truck or care if I was alone and would be forever. I didn't want to face my family or even the friends I have now. It was my fault. I brought all the pain to the people I knew, including Rachel and myself. I cried until I had no more tears. I cried a river and then I was left with nothing, with nobody to accept who I am, to forgive me for what I did. I am alone. I use to not mind, but now I've lost who even I myself am.

Then I sank, I fell to the once dew covered ground and hugged my knees. I closed my eyes. Then it was all over.

Chapter Twenty-one

The next morning, I woke up to Andrew yanking the covers off my bed, "Get up! We have school. It is Wednesday!"

"Go away!" I snapped at him and pulled my sheets back up to wrap up in them again. My eyes were so swollen from the crying that I couldn't open them.My stomach felt empty and the last thing I wanted to do was go to school and pretend everything was alright. I didn't want to burden my friends nor did I want Cameron or Tyler to think I am weak and pathetic. I had learn nothing. It is better to skip school than get all failing grades.

"Leave her alone Andrew," Mom said, as she walked in. Isn't that perfect? The one and only mother to ever find her daughter passed out from exhaustion on the ground of a house that she used to call   home.
Now she will probably try to persuade me into going on with life because it's important. She's probably the Mother who would still drag you out the door and force you to attend school because nothing else is more important.

That is always the Mother she has been, but something in her had changed. She sat on the right side of my bed and faced me. Her blue eyes looked saddened and she herself seemed to slump over, like it was not important to go to work or that everything she had done was pointless. That was just like how I felt yesterday. That today was worse.

Instead my mom didn't try to talk me into anything. She just sat there with a blank stare to her face as if aliens came down to plant earth. As if some magician were hitmatizing her. That's when I thought it good to speak. Not that I wanted to, that was something I thought I'd never want to do again but she looked so awful. Her hair wasn't brushed, her face without make-up and it looked like she hasn't gotten sleep in a week. That is probably what I look like too.

"Mom?"

"You can stay home today," she said, with the same blank look as she turned her head to me. Then she squeezed my hand and in a daze, I walked to my room.

It no longer felt like a room, but a prison. All I could think about was how I had done that to my family, how I put the Hall family in that situation and how I ruined my brother's senior year in high school. My room felt like a closed space with no freedom or room for escape. It seemed like an empty bubble, which rejected any happy thoughts. It felt like a prison, a jail cell keeping me in and stealing my oxygen, which the lack of, was closing in around me.

Chapter Twenty-two

Wait what?

He did he did that to all of us?!

I don't believe it!

Ask him.

I had been texting Sydney that Thursday. The week passed slowly. I had been in bed, crying for the past three days. My mom stayed home too. She often came upstairs to check on me. I tried not to turn away from her when she checked my head for temperature or anything else that would give her signs of my being sick or head trauma issues. I'd been assuring her I felt okay physically, but she never bought into it.

Finally, Sydney at least decided to text me and see if I was doing okay. Sydney told me that my friends had been wondering where I was. I didn't tell her that it was my fault the house was gone or that I had a major breakdown Monday. I didn't tell her I felt empty. If at all possible, I might be able to keep the conversation going, just to talk to someone not in my household. However, I tried to direct all conversations away from me. In this case, we ended up talking about Cameron. She told me everything. Sydney told me that they excluded Cameron from the group because of what he did. It blew me out of the water. I really had no clue people my age actually did things like that.

Apparently, Cameron had gotten this specific group of friends to go racing on some dirt roads for fun on the weekends. It was all good, since they had a fun time. That is, until Cameron left them. One truck had tumbled into a ditch and people were injured.   It turns out they had to call the police, but got fined for trespassing.   Cameron was in a different truck with Tanner when the others rolled over.   There was another truck too, but they stayed and helped.   It wasn't only Shasta, Sydney, Miles, and James, but Tyler and Tanner too.   Cameron had abandoned them.

That's why Tyler had been saying those awful things to me about Cameron and that's why he said that Cameron was good for leaving people.   I didn't know Cameron would abandon his friends like that, especially to save his own skin.

If I have learned one lesson about who destroyed my home, which was me, it is that you can't judge someone.   You can't make assumptions that are most likely wrong anyway.

I had the assumption that it was Dustin who destroyed my life, who attacked me, when really it was all me.   I'd done it to myself.   I had set myself up for failure.   I excluded myself.   It was all me.

So I didn't judge Cameron.   I just wanted to help.

★★★

"Hey you!"

"What are you doing here?"

I asked, and scrambled under my covers.   Cameron is in my house! Who let him in? Who told him I wanted to see him anyway?

"Um, I was just coming to check on you.   You've missed school and you aren't even in pain-

"Don't say that to me!" I said my voice muffled by the sheets.

Don't make assumptions Cam.

"Okay, I'm sorry I wanted to see how you were doing...I'm really sorry about your house, Em."

"How do you know about that?"

"Andrew told me."

I rolled my eyes, not that anyone could see me.   It just felt necessary.

124

"Embril please, I don't think of you any differently. It isn't your fault. Everyone forgets things."

How does he do this? Every time Cameron tries to cheer me up, it doesn't take much. How did he know my biggest fear…that people would think of me badly, or that something I've done, who I am or what I look like, could change the way someone thinks of me in a bad way? Is my fear not something that is only me? Am I not abnormal? Do others feel this way? Is my fear more common than I had thought? It must be. He's my perfect friend, and right now I want to be exactly like him.

Instead of saying anything, I pulled my sheets back up to right under my chin and just looked at him.

"What?" He tried to get me to say something but I couldn't. I had no words. I did not want to see Cameron in the first place. I didn't want him to see me this way, all depressed like I was. I didn't want to face him for changing his life, for having to put up with me. Shoot, if I had known it was my fault, I would have never met Cameron. I would have never met Shasta or James. I wouldn't even know Tyler's name.

If it weren't for my mistake, I'd still be lonely. I would still be convinced that no one needs friends to live, to really live; and that's when I thought of what Cameron did. Those were his friends, his group, his people. That was his social life. He made one mistake and they erupted like volcanoes. This is what causes my fear, that people will look at you differently and think of you as a whole new person they don't see any worth in. This is what has caused me to learn that people need friends; that people helping other people is what America is asll about. I need to help Cameron. I need his friends…*my* friends to see the truth.

Cameron then realized it was silent. He climbed into the bed beside me and I was happy. I was glad to see that someone cares, that someone, *anyone* would put the smallest bit of my feelings before their own. I was glad that he would do about anything I asked him

to do. I would do it for him, even if I am a coward.
I would man up to do whatever he needed me for.
"Cameron?"
"Yes Em?"
"I love you."
"I know. I love you too."
"You know why our friends are mad at you?" I
asked, hoping that I didn't make him mad.
"Um, yeah. You do?"
"Well...Sydney told me."
"Perfect," Cameron's voice started to sound
irritated.
"We need to talk to them. You made one mistake
just like I did. I believe they don't have the right to
exclude you."
"Embril, there is no need for you to get involved in
my life. You have your own problems to deal with-
"Excuse me?" I had to butt in but he ignored me.
"I have mine, let me live my life as I may. Please
just stay out of it." Cameron started to get mad, his
voice rose the more he talked.
"Look, you had to go get into mine-
"Embril, I had to I knew I had no potential in
getting my friends back, you did. You needed my
help. I changed your life."
"And I changed yours. Cameron, I'm just trying
to help. I do see potential for you to have friends
again, the same friends that turned their back on you.
"They didn't, I turned my back on them. Embril,
I just told you to not interfere. Why are you still
talking! Don't you have something to fix in your own
life, like for say, apologizing to your family?"
Cameron threw his arms up and stepped away from
me. I never thought I could stand seeing him yell at
me, seeing him be mad, but I had no choice, this was
different. Cameron was accusing me for trying to
help. For crying out loud, he needs me like I needed
him without knowing I needed him. It's about the
same situation and he wouldn't even let me get a word
out. If he would listen he would understand.

"Would you listen for one second?" that's when my voice rose, because that's when I had it. All I wanted was for him to listen and try to understand. That's when Andrew walked in the door. He didn't give it a second glance. Andrew took Cameron by the shoulders and escorted him from the door. I'm surprised that Cameron didn't try to speak his mind while he was forced to leave by my brother.

It was quiet again, my room grew cold. I started to feel empty, but tried my best to push that feeling away. I don't care what Cameron just said. I know that I should just stay out of it, but he needs to understand that I can't sit by and watch him be lonely. Apparently, he had no choice to butt into my business. Well neither do I.

Chapter Twenty-three

I ended up going to school the next day, on Friday. I know I should have just skipped, but really, I couldn't stand staying at home another day; not because I was getting tried of being at my new home, well actually, that was part of it, but because I'm on a mission. It was my fault that I burnt down the house and it was my fault I changed Cameron's life. I'm going to fix my faults. I will rewind my mistake, hoping I will feel better about what I did. I *had* to fix at least one thing that leads to my mistake.

"Ah, I thought you would stay home today," Andrew commented as I climbed into the passenger seat of his truck.

"Don't judge," Is all I said. If I can spread my lesson to other people, the town might be a little better place for a teenager to live.

We weren't really quiet on the way to school. Andrew turned the radio up and it turned out that Big and Rich were playing. To be completely truthful, Andrew and I used to jam to those songs. We would turn it on in his room and jump on his bed attempting to sing the lyrics.

We still knew the words many years later. I think he was even glad to see me as myself again. Sure, it was a Friday, but I felt alive. I felt that I could do this. I could help Cameron. I could help everyone.

Then we pulled up to the parking lot. There were a lot of people already there, so I guess we arrived later than usual. Andrew parked the truck as I checked the time. We had fifteen minutes!

"Andrew have you been here this late everyday?"

"Um...."

I could tell that he didn't really want to give me an answer so I sighed and opened the truck door and lifted my back pack to the seat. It was also heavier than normal. Maybe It's just a first-day-back thing.

Then I put my key chain around my neck and heard someone yell my name from a distance.

"Hey! Hey Embril, come over here, quick!"

It was James. He was only straight across the road from me.   It couldn't hurt my timing to go over to him, so I shut my door and jogged to Tanners vehicle before other cars flew by.

"What?" I asked.

"Do you know where Cameron is?"

"No, why?"

"We were going to ask where he was last night. We asked him if he was planning on going to the carnival and he said 'Yeah', but we didn't see him there."

"Oh, maybe he had something more important to do at the last minute. Why did you want to know if he'd be there?"

"Top secret," he winked at me.

I would have pressed the question until he told me but I hate being late to class.

I didn't say anything else.   I simply turned away from him and walked back to Andrew's truck.

I thought of what James said on my way back. Could they possibly want to hurt him any further? The only thing I could think of was that they were planning on pulling a prank on him.

Andrew seemed to have already gone inside.   I pulled on the handle to get my back pack out but nothing happened.

"Oh no, no no no no no!"

Andrew had locked it.   He thought I had everything out, so he pressed the lock button.   I need in there! I need my thing… my notebook, my jacket, I don't even have a pencil!

I looked around the lot.   There were still people outside but I didn't know how anyone could help me.

Then I spotted the cops.   The thing is…they were way over by the entrance.   If I wanted to get to them that badly, I would have to walk.   There's no point to ask a buddy to drive me over there.   I'd never ask

someone to be late to school for me, because I had forgotten my key, unless it was urgent. All I did was forget something and I have to get put down for it!
Its not my fault. Someone might say that I have no excuse, but I really did forget.

So I started my walk. It took me a while and after I got to my destination, students ran inside leaving the parking lot vacant.

Thankfully, the policemen drove me to Andrew's truck after I told him what had happened. When he parked the car in the spot next to Andrew's, he started laughing. It wasn't a small quiet laugh, he really was laughing at me.

"What?" I asked. When he didn't answer I grew irritated.

"What? Tell me, what is so funny?"

"Miss, you have a key to the truck," he said, still laughing, but I heard him clear enough.

"Well, no it's in my back pack inside the vehicle!"

"Don't get angry, but isn't this it... around your neck?" The policemen had finally stopped laughing, his expression having changed to sympathy. Then he pointed to my key chain.

My key chain...I completely forgot something else? You are right! I grabbed my key before I shutting the door, with a red face. Why do I forget things all the time?

"Right, well thank you," I quickly said, as I got out of the car. Thinking it might be best to ask for a slip, I asked, "Sir, do you mind if I can ask you for an excuse slip? I'm afraid that I'm late for class."

The policemen nodded and wrote something down on a slip of paper. When he was finished I took it and said thank you.

Really, I wish I could have remembered my key. It was on me the entire time and now I'm late for class. Seriously, I don't care if it is excused or unexcused. I hate walking in late in general. People stare at you for no particular reason. Teachers might question you and then you have to jump into the lesson and try to understand what it is the teachers are talking about. It's the most hated thing I can think of when it comes to school.

★★★

By lunch time, I had already thought up a plan to get my friends to become one group again. It was a plan that would make it easier for them to forgive Cameron.

"Hey, you want to sit with me today? I'm a little lonely," I said, hoping that Sydney would agree. It also felt necessary to speak the last sentence. If I really didn't need her there I think she would have denied my request.

I ran around the cafeteria searching for my other friends, they all said yes.

It was good that Cameron was the first to the table, because if he knew what I was doing, he wouldn't sit there. He might have chosen to go back to his classroom, or worse, to the bathroom.

"Hey," I said to Cameron, as I sat down. The others hesitated, while looking at each other before looking at me, then glancing lastly to Cameron. Could all of my friends really feel the same hatred for Cameron? It was one big mistake.

My friends decided to sit down anyway. I gave them time to understand the situation, to get use to being next to Cameron again, before I spoke.

"So...I'm concerned," I started, staring at my half eaten apple.

"About what?" Miles asked.

"Well, it occurs to me that I have made a mistake." I think that it would be the best choice to explain what I just went through and the lesson I learned. Perhaps they would understand better from hearing a different story, and then put it into the perspective of what they did to Cameron.

"Monday, I went back to my house," I glanced at Cameron and I shouldn't have because he rolled his eyes. Starting again, "I went to get my truck but then

132

I decided I wanted to know the cause of my house burning down so I asked some firefighters to do some investigating. I found out that it was me. It was my fault."

"That day I broke. It was me who destroyed my family's things, it was me who ruined my brother's last year in high school." I saw Cameron jump and raise his hand as if to protest, but I didn't give him a chance. "I also learned not to judge people or make assumptions. Really, I blamed someone else, someone who attacked me in Wal-Mart. I thought he was trying to tear me and my family down. It was my fault."

"So I just wanted to let you know that it was wrong for me to make an assumption on a thing that didn't add up." I let my story sink in for a second or two. I wanted my friends to really understand.

"I'm sorry," Shasta said and that's when I knew it was okay to talk again.

"Its okay, I just think you guys should see if you have been judging and making actions, like what happened with Cameron a year ago....maybe thought something different."

"I agree," Tanner was the first to speak.

"Me too," said Shasta. The others were silent for a more than enough time. It was like they were really mad at him...until they all looked into it.

People were saying I agree and that made my lips turn up into a smile. I had done it, I tied one mistake together. I fixed something!

"So who wants to go to the carnival tonight?" James asked.

I gave him a glare, was he really the one to ask this question?

"No pranks?" I had to make sure.

"What? No of course not," he said, offended.

So the day went on. We talked about random things until the bell rang. We were a group of friends and I had fixed it. I had no idea that I could change something that important. That time of the day made

everything so much better. We laughed at our peers
stupidity and we had a group hug before we left the
premises.

Chapter Twenty-four

That night, we went to the carnival. We all went...
Shasta, Sydney, Miles, James, Cameron, Tanner, me,
and even Tyler. Tyler Einstein was the person who it
really took a lot of effort to get to forgive someone else,
especially because he seemed hurt the most by it. In
my opinion, it seemed to me that since he couldn't
change the group's mind back, he didn't have a story
that compared to mine so he gave up.

"I will get the tickets. Who has the food?"
Cameron asked. I was glad to see him actually
involved. It made me happy to realize that he wasn't
mad at me anymore for getting into his life, but it
wasn't just his life. I think we all are a lot happier this
way.

"I got food!" James said which made me laugh
because he looked way too excited.

"Okay, meet you at the Ferris Wheel... go!"
Cameron said and we dashed away from each other.
Miles and Tanner went with James to get the food,
and Tyler went with Shasta and Sydney to wait at the
Ferris Wheel, but I chose neither. It isn't that I
wanted to be alone, that would have meant that I was
excluding myself again and the last time I did that, it
was torture. Instead, I walked with Cameron.

"Are you still mad at me?" I asked.

"No, actually, I wanted to thank you . I was not in
my right mind yesterday."

"So we're good?"

"We are good," he established.

The line for tickets was about the same length as
the food line. It would be clear that one part of the
group would get through at the same time the other
half was. It timed out perfectly. That's when my
thoughts scattered.

First, I thought about when I was younger and how
I knew I would be just fine without anyone to talk to.
Secondly, I though about how I broke down because

everything was my fault.   Even fixing something was my fault.   Not everything has to be bad when someone uses that phrase. Finally, I thought about Cameron and my other friends.   I thought of how I wanted each of them to be happy, that I wanted each of them to see what it is like to have friends, because it is everything to me.   It is completely different from not having any.   I thought how I use to think friends would be useless, but truly, they aren't bad, it' s far from bad.

"Cameron I have one last thing to say."
He looked straight at me and waited, "You aren't so bad."

Acknowledgements

I want to say thank you to my Pa Paw first, because he is the person who inspired me to become a writer. We neither one did not know how far I would come into the writing career but it has helped me in so many ways. It was one day when I was in fourth grade that I came home and said, "I want to write but I don't know what to write." My Pa Paw then told me to write a story and I thought it was a good idea. Thank you Pa Paw, I love you so much.

I also want to say thank you to my Nanny who made me laugh and gave me great ideas for small details of my stories. I want to thank her for the support of my books and for wanting to edit everything I wrote. I love you.

Thanks to my ninth grade English teacher, Mr. Hammer. He has read the short and the long stories I have created and I want to say thank you for helping with my grammar.

I want to thank all the people who have come into my life, my acquaintances and my friends, because they have helped me become who I really am and they are the ones who inspired me to write a book about friends in the first place.

Most importantly, thank you to all my readers that have picked up this book. You took the time out of your day to give my book a chance and that means a lot to me. I hope you enjoyed the story.

Remember to always realize what is fictional and what is reality.

www.ingramcontent.com/pod-product-compliance
Lightning Source LLC
Chambersburg PA
CBHW051459050726
47593CB00005B/2134